"Do you like it?" Scott asked.

In an instant, Rena was on her knees beside the cradle, running her hand along the curves of the wood. "Like it? It's perfect."

He laughed. "It's hardly perfect. It's not even finished. Be careful not to get a splinter." He pulled her hand away from the rough wood.

She looked up at him. "Will you put it in my room when you finish?" The hope in her eyes was all the thanks he could ever want for his labor.

"Of course." He realized he still held her hand. "The hard part is over. Only the fine work is left to do."

The cradle gave tangible evidence of the impending arrival of the baby…another man's baby. Scott had built his home with every intention of marrying and raising a family to carry his name and tend his land for centuries to come. Louise's betrayal had killed that dream.

Tonight, he would bury it in the sawdust at his feet, while he sanded off the rough edges of a cradle he'd built for the child of another man.

Angel Moore fell in love with romance in elementary school when she read the story of Robin Hood and Maid Marian. Who doesn't want to escape to a happily-ever-after world? Married to her best friend, she has two wonderful sons, a lovely daughter-in-law and three grandkids. She loves sharing her faith and the hope she knows is real because of God's goodness to her. Find her at www.angelmoorebooks.com.

Books by Angel Moore

Love Inspired Historical

Conveniently Wed
The Marriage Bargain
The Rightful Heir
Husband by Arrangement

ANGEL MOORE

Husband by Arrangement

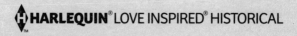

HARLEQUIN® LOVE INSPIRED® HISTORICAL

Recycling programs
for this product may
not exist in your area.

LOVE INSPIRED BOOKS

ISBN-13: 978-1-335-36961-1

Husband by Arrangement

www.Harlequin.com

Printed in U.S.A.

There is therefore now no condemnation to them which are in Christ Jesus, who walk not after the flesh, but after the Spirit.
—*Romans* 8:1

To my editor, Dina Davis.
Thank you for helping me remember to write with joy.

To my readers, for inspiring me to keep writing.

And to God, my source and strength.

Chapter One

Gran Colina, Texas
December 1881

Rena Livingston hung her head. She couldn't look at Sheriff Scott Braden. Not while her father was asking him to marry her and give her unborn child a name.

"I'd be beholden to you for the rest of my days if you do this for my Rena." Her father's voice wasn't boisterous or bold like when he gave speeches as the mayor of Gran Colina. It was heavy with sorrow. And it was her fault.

"Oscar, you know I'd do anything in the world for you. I owe you my life, but this is too much." Rena could feel the sheriff's eyes on her now. She saw his hand as he swept it in her direction. "Why, Rena doesn't even like me."

She cringed. Scott Braden had become one of her father's closest friends right after he'd moved to Gran Colina two years ago. She'd never forget the day they'd met. Bank robbers had burst into the Gran Colina Bank and Trust. Scott had shoved her under a desk to keep her out of harm's way. Only she hadn't realized what was happening. Her outburst at his actions had distracted him and nearly cost Scott his life. When he'd tried to quieten her, one of the robbers had put a pistol to his head. The man would have pulled the trigger if her father hadn't knocked the gun away. Scott and her father had subdued the robbers in the struggle that followed. The events of that day got Scott the job as sheriff and sealed the friendship between the two men.

But Rena always bristled in Scott's presence. Something about the man was unsettling. It wasn't his strong good looks. Blue eyes so clear the sky should be jealous. His full bottom lip lifted on one side as it made its way to the corner of his mouth. To some it would appear as a defect, but on Scott, it was as if he'd been created with so much perfection that the one little offset prevented him from being flawless. Those looks gave him trouble of a different kind from the single ladies in town. They were always bringing him pies or dinner, hoping to win his attention. To no avail.

No. Her discomfort around him was relentless. If she were honest with herself, she'd admit that the times he'd suggested she should attend church with her father had made her feel judged by him. If he'd thought poorly of her character before, her situation would validate those thoughts.

Even in her current state of humiliation, she was compelled to speak. "I told you this wouldn't work, Papa."

"Be silent, Rena. You have forfeited your right to have a say in these matters." Her father never spoke to her so harshly, but she'd broken his heart. If possible, the events of today had wounded him more than when she'd stopped attending church with him after her mother had died four years ago. She'd felt so alone without Momma. The pain she endured now was like then. Oh, how she missed the comfort and wisdom of her mother in difficult times.

"Now, Oscar, the girl oughta have a say in her future." Scott's defense of her was unexpected. So much so that she lifted her face to meet his eyes. "I know you're dealing with a serious situation, but it is Rena's life." She swallowed when his words made her want to smile in gratitude.

But Papa was right. She had no reason to speak against anything he tried to do to help her.

"It's not just about her. If word of her—" her father cleared his throat "—condition gets out, there will be a scandal. The likes of which we haven't seen in the leadership of Gran Colina since you and I worked so hard to get crime under control and make this town a safe place for people to settle." He shook his head. "And with the election coming up in just three months, we could both lose our jobs."

This sentence caused Scott to drop onto the edge of the settee. He'd jumped to his feet at her father's initial request. She could see the fight drain out of him as he considered the possibility of losing his badge.

"I'm truly sorry, Papa." She wouldn't cry. Not in front of Scott.

Her father didn't look at her. He'd barely looked at her since she'd told him what happened. "Sorrow is good for your soul, but it won't fix your future. We have to act now."

Scott turned to her. "Are you certain?"

She couldn't pretend she didn't know he was asking about the child. She lowered her gaze and nodded. Nothing could force her to vocalize the truth again today. Within an hour of telling her father at breakfast, he'd summoned the sheriff and put his plan in motion. Only the plan had stalled with Scott's resistance.

Her father spoke again. "I'll need your promise that you won't share a word of what we've discussed. I'm not sure who I'll find to step up at this point." He shook his head. "If only I had more time. But there's just no one else I'd trust to know this."

Rena had waited to tell her father until she was certain Eugene Rodgers wasn't coming back. A postcard had arrived the day before. A pretty drawing of a big city in California covered one side. The other side held a bold, scribbled note. It was the only time she'd heard from him in the two months since he'd left her and Gran Colina.

Signed on as a seaman leaving for Alaska tonight. I wish you a happy life. My short time in Gran Colina will always be a fond memory, but the world is big, and I wish to explore it.

Her hope that he would return and make an honest woman of her was gone. It was sailing across the Pacific to places unknown.

Scott asked, "Is there no aunt in the East or cousin in Florida to give you a home?"

"There is not." Rena forced the words out with torturous effort. "I'd have preferred that to imposing on you, but Papa is my only living relative."

"Is there no chance that the father will do his duty by you?"

"None. He is gone forever."

It was clear to her now that Eugene had wanted to keep their engagement secret because he'd had no intention of marrying her. No one, not even her closest friend, had known they were seeing one another.

He'd convinced Rena that their marriage would take place the following morning. No one would know they'd been together. His smooth words had led her foolish mind to accept and trust him.

Oscar said, "She told me it was that wretched Rodgers fella." He clinched his fists at his side. "He gave her his promise."

"Papa, don't. If I'd lived the way you and Momma taught me—" She paused, garnering the courage to continue. "It's my own fault."

Shame covered her soul. Why had she believed Eugene? How had she allowed herself to be so stupid?

"Eugene Rodgers?" Scott ground his teeth at the memory of the young man with slick manners. "I was glad to see him get on the train the day he left Gran Colina. I had no idea he was running from his responsibilities." He'd disliked the man on sight. Those sly ways and pretty words could woo a woman, but Scott had been leery of him from the start. He should have paid closer attention. Maybe he could have prevented this situation if he had.

Rena's next words surprised him. "He didn't know about the child."

"You kept it from him? A man has a right to know about his own flesh and blood. Have you written to inform him?" He would be hard-pressed to forgive such a thing if it happened to him. A child deserved a father. One to love and provide for their needs.

"I didn't know he was leaving. He left me no way to contact him." She shook her head and didn't look at him. "He left the morning after..." She choked on her words and didn't finish.

"Have you heard from him since he left?"

"Only a postcard saying he won't be back and has gone to see the world."

Scott wanted to find Rodgers and drag him back. He should never have left Rena like this. But a man like that would be untraceable—and unworthy of a good wife and a child.

There were several men in Gran Colina who would be glad to take Rena on as their wife. Men who wouldn't appreciate her stubborn ways or determined mind. And if they knew about the child, she could be treated poorly.

No woman deserved that. Not even after so obvious a sin.

"Rena, what do you think of your father's proposition?" She sat with her arms crossed and her face taut. The green eyes that often held laughter and mischief were sober. Her dimples made no appearance. Not even the childlike freckles from her youth softened the sorrow in her countenance today.

Her voice was low, but steady, as she answered. "I have presented him with an impossible situation, and he is trying to protect me. As well as everything he's done to improve Gran Colina. If scandal breaks out now, he'll lose the election for sure."

As much as he hated to admit it, she was right. "Do you wish to marry?"

"It was my fondest wish before—" She held his gaze. He knew she chose her words with care. "I know it is best for my father and my child. And for myself. It is not how I ever intended for my life to unfold." The straight set of her pink mouth reinforced the sincerity of her answer.

Oscar said, "I don't see any alternative. You are the best choice, Scott. The only choice, actually. Anyone else could use this to undermine my work as mayor. You remember how unruly Gran Colina was when you first came to town. All our work could be undone in a matter of weeks if this isn't handled discreetly."

"Oscar, will you leave us to speak privately?"

The mayor seemed to have aged overnight. He looked from Rena and back to Scott. "I'll go out to the kitchen and make us some coffee."

When he left them alone in the front room, Scott turned to Rena. Her slim neck was stiff. "Are you well? You look as though you've lost weight."

"I am healthy, but food holds no appeal to me at the moment."

"What shall we do?"

One eyebrow lifted. "It's more a question of what you will do. I'm not in a position to make demands."

"There's something we need to talk about before I agree to this arrangement."

She didn't speak, but the widening of her eyes spoke of fear that he'd refuse her.

"You know I'm a believer in the Lord above."

Rena nodded.

"And you? I've seen you in services on Sundays for the last couple of months, but we've never talked about your beliefs."

"I walked away from the church and God when my mother died. I was so hurt. I wish I'd stayed there beside my father." She wrung her hands together in her lap. "He's a good man, but he was so lonely without Momma, and I couldn't just accept that Momma was gone. Not after how I'd prayed for God to spare her. It was a foolish choice."

"Have you asked the Good Lord to forgive you?"

She nodded. "I have." She raised tear-filled eyes to meet his gaze. "I know there are hard days ahead for me, but I'm determined to face them with God. I made a mess of things when I didn't heed His ways."

"That's all I needed to hear. The rest isn't mine to know. We can marry immediately if you choose."

"Really? How can you say that's all you need to know?"

"Jesus does the forgiving. You've done me no wrong. Jesus even said for the people without sin to cast the first stone."

The tears dripped off her lashes, and she dashed them away with the back of her hand. "Still, I'm powerful sorry."

"Then the next step will be to forgive yourself. Making things right with God and living your life by the Good Book—that's where you'll find your hope."

"I don't know what to say."

"I can give you and your little one my name. Only God can give you peace."

"What about your life? Why would you be willing to give up your future for me? Knowing what you know."

"My future is being the sheriff of Gran Colina. But if your father loses the mayor's race, I'm likely to lose, too. I know I was only elected because your father told everyone he could about the bank robbery he and I thwarted. No matter how it happened, it's who I am now."

"You have your homestead."

"Since my sister married and moved away, it's all I can do to keep up with that and being sheriff. She cooked and cleaned. Things I don't have the time or talent for."

"That doesn't seem like a fair deal to me. You save my reputation, and all I have to do is housework. What if you meet someone and fall in love?"

A dull ache in his chest quivered for a brief moment and stilled. "You won't ever have to worry about me falling in love. I gave up on that notion a long time ago."

Two hours later, Scott stood beside Rena at the altar

of Gran Colina Church. He rubbed his palm down the side of his Sunday trousers before taking Rena's hand from Oscar. Reverend Walter Gillis began the ceremony that would take away any freedom Scott had. The reverend asked him to repeat the vows and put a ring on Rena's finger. He pledged all his earthly possessions to her, but he had no ring. She lowered her eyes to the floor when his voice wavered as he promised to love and honor her. He would love her. Like a sister in Christ. But he'd never love any woman for himself. Not again.

"You may kiss the bride." Reverend Gillis's words hung in the air.

They'd agreed before coming to the church that no one was to know their marriage wasn't one of mutual agreement and love. Only Scott, Rena and Oscar would ever know. Scott was quite sure Rena hadn't considered a kiss to seal their vows when they'd decided that.

He certainly had not. He froze. If he tried to kiss her, she might burst into tears. The strain of the day had taken a toll on him. Only God knew how she was holding up.

Rena lifted her face to him. The pleading in her eyes told him they needed to complete the picture of a happy couple or their arrangement would never be believed.

He placed one finger under her chin and saw her jaw tighten. He turned her face slightly away from the friends who'd gathered to witness the event. The kiss he placed on her cheek was so close to her lips that no one would question his actions, but the near miss of her mouth protected her from questioning his intentions.

The softness of her skin contradicted the pain in her. He prayed they would be able to build a life together for the sake of her child and her father. It was inexcusable that Eugene Rodgers had taken advantage of Rena. The scoundrel would never know about the baby. Scott couldn't understand such a man. No child of his would ever be raised by another man. Not as long as he had breath in his body.

Of course, that would never happen. Watching his fiancée, Louise Kinard, walk away from their engagement to marry Thomas Freeman, the town banker, over a year ago had taught Scott that women wanted a smooth talker. Even if the man promised things he would never deliver, women were fascinated by fancy and unimpressed by a solid man with a good heart and a loyal nature.

If his sister hadn't moved away and left him struggling to keep his homestead going, he didn't think he'd be standing here now, kissing Rena.

But he was. And now all of Gran Colina would know that the sheriff had married the mayor's daughter. Before summer's end they'd welcome a new life into the world.

Lord, help me to adjust to all of this by then. And help Rena, too.

Saving Gran Colina from falling backward into lawlessness was a noble goal. With Thomas Freeman using all his polished ways to run for mayor against Oscar in the coming election, and Gilbert Jefferson running for his former position as sheriff, everything they'd accomplished was at risk.

Scott had already given himself fully to protecting Gran Colina. He hoped Rena would settle into their new life without regret. If she couldn't, or if word got out that she was carrying another man's child, their whole scheme might be for naught.

Suddenly it was all over, and Oscar was pumping his hand. "Congratulations, Scott." The man's eyes held gratitude that couldn't be expressed in front of the people who gathered around the new couple.

"Thank you, sir." Scott shook hands with Reverend Gillis and then his wife, Mildred. While everyone pressed in on them to offer happy wishes, Rena seemed to become more and more tense. The smile she wore appeared genuine, but he was concerned about how long she could keep up the pretense of wedded bliss.

Rena's closest friend, Charlotte Green, spoke quietly into her ear, and Rena nodded. Scott wondered if Charlotte knew the truth. He hoped not. Charlotte stepped back, and her hand fell away from Rena's arm.

"Congratulations, Sheriff," Charlotte said. "I must say I'm surprised by this turn of events, but I do wish you well. Rena is a dear friend. Her happiness is important to me. See that you do right by her." Her grin let him know she was pleased for her friend.

"Thank you." He smiled what he hoped was a genuine smile. "I'll do my best."

Rena accepted a hug from the preacher's wife. "Thank you, Mrs. Gillis."

"You've made such a wonderful choice. I just know

you and the sheriff will have a happy life." Mildred Gillis's round face crinkled with her smile. "Oh, the joy this must bring to your father. And to think the two of you have kept your courtship a secret. You are a sly one." Light laughter punctuated her words, but Scott saw the pain they brought to Rena.

He stepped closer to her and raised his voice to address the gathering. "Thank you all for coming on such short notice, but if you don't mind, I'd like for us to be on our way. We want to be home before dark."

Chuckles came from the small crowd as they parted to give him and Rena room to leave the church. He looped Rena's hand into the crook of his elbow and led her outside.

She took a deep breath when they passed through the doors and pulled her hand free of his arm. "Thank you. It was getting to be a bit much."

"It's been quite a day." He offered his hand to assist her into his wagon. She released it as soon as she was seated. The walk around the back of the wagon gave him another moment to whisper a prayer. He was in a marriage he'd never expected, to a woman who didn't love or want him. A woman he'd never have chosen. Prayer had always been a part of his life. He imagined it was about to become a constant thing.

Scott climbed aboard and lifted the reins. The two miles to his homestead never seemed so long. The afternoon was brisk, and Rena pulled the top of her cape closer around her neck.

"There's a blanket under your seat."

"I'm fine, thank you." She didn't look at him.

Not another word was spoken until they arrived at his home.

Their home.

He set the brake and turned to her. "It's not what you're used to. The house and barn are done, but I want to expand the corral." He lifted his arm to point beyond her. "There's a good-sized garden there. Not much to it at this time of year. There's plenty of meat in the smokehouse, and Ann did a lot of canning before she married. I made her take what she could with her." He vaulted over the wheel onto the ground. "I thought I'd be on my own. We'll buy what we need in town until spring."

He walked around to help her from the wagon. She lost her footing, and he had to catch her by the waist and set her on the ground. She stepped away from him the instant she regained her balance. Her movements were so abrupt that he apologized.

The set of her mouth had only softened for the ceremony. It had returned to testify to her determination. "If you'll show me where to unpack my valise, I'll see to supper."

He nodded and lifted her case from the back of the wagon. She followed him up the steps to the porch, and he opened the door. "After you."

Rena's back was straight, and her shoulders were square as she entered his house. She came to a stop just inside the dim interior and gasped.

Scott scooted around her and dropped her valise near the door. Not until this moment did he remember the state of the house. Without Ann's help, he'd done only a minimal amount of cleaning. When he'd left for town this morning, there had been no idea of someone coming back with him this evening.

He went to the fireplace and struck a match against the hearth to light the fire and then a lamp. He adjusted the wick and lifted the lamp so she could see the room.

Tears swam in her eyes. He knew she wouldn't let them fall, but he hated to add the disorder of his home to the chaos of her life today.

In spite of her predicament, he wanted to make the best of their arrangement. The house was proof that he needed someone to help him. "It's not as bad as it seems. I promise. We can get it set in order and make it work."

He hoped the words were true of more than his house.

Chapter Two

Rena stood in the middle of the room trying to take in the magnitude of disorder one man could bring to a space. The mess of his home paled in comparison to the mess she'd made of her life.

At that exact moment, her body reacted to the child she was carrying in a now-too-familiar fashion. She turned on her heel and sped through the door and around to the side of the house.

It was several minutes before she climbed the porch steps and reentered her new home. Much of the clutter that had greeted her earlier was in a pile near the door on the back wall, and Scott was sweeping the floor.

"You shouldn't be sweeping. That's my responsibility now." She unbuttoned the top of her wool cape and slipped it off her shoulders.

"I made this mess. It's not fair for you to clean it up."

Rena raised her eyebrows. "Really? Isn't that what you're doing for me?"

He stopped short and stared at her. "That's hardly the same thing."

"You're right." She held out her hand for the broom. "What you're doing for me—and my child—is much more important than sweeping up." She grasped the top of the broom handle. "Please let me do my part. It's difficult enough to be beholden to you. At least let me help."

He released the broom. "I promise to do better. I've been a bit overwhelmed since Ann left. I didn't realize how much work she did until she was gone."

Rena swept dust from the corner behind the door. "Let me guess. You thought that because she owned a shop and spent her days in town she didn't contribute much to the chores." She opened the door and tossed the small rug from the entryway onto the porch. A cloud of dust rose up and blew away in the winter breeze.

"I'll get the other rugs." Scott rolled up the braided rug in front of the fireplace and added it to the one she'd tossed outside.

"I can do it. You need to see to the team and feed the animals. I'll take care of the house." She pulled back the curtain on the front window and realized, from the amount of dust and ash gathered on the sill, that it would take her several days to get the house thoroughly clean. "I won't do it all today, but by the end of next week, things should be in good order."

Scott brushed his hands together to remove the dust of the rug and immediately apologized when he saw it float to the floor she'd swept moments before.

Rena shook her head. "Don't worry about it. Papa never has learned to brush his feet outside."

"We'll get it sorted out." He looked at the room and then over his shoulder at the team and wagon. "I'll take care of the outside chores and come back to help with supper."

"That's not necessary." She tackled the dirt on the floor in front of the fireplace with the broom.

"I insist. We've both had quite a day, and I am accustomed to taking care of myself."

She stopped and laughed. An honest, hearty laugh. "I can see that." She opened her arms wide to indicate the room.

He smiled at her sarcasm. "It's nice to see you laugh." He closed the door, and she listened as his boots crossed the porch and descended the steps.

When she heard the wagon pull away from the house, she dropped onto the chair by the hearth. "What a mess you've gotten yourself into, Rena Livingston." As the words left her lips, she realized she was Rena Braden now.

Nothing of her former self remained. Eugene Rodgers had left her with a child and taken everything else from her. Not even her father recognized who she had become.

Being secretly engaged to a man who'd traveled the country had been thrilling. At first. She'd gone from excitement to shame and finally to disbelief and dread when Eugene had left. Wallowing in self-pity hadn't helped. She'd had no choice but to move forward. One day at a time. One step at a time.

Lord, give me strength.

She forced herself out of the chair and explored the house. By the time Scott returned, she had ham frying on the stove and the table cleaned and set for a modest supper.

Scott took off his hat and hung it on a peg by the door. "That smells nice."

"It's the best I could do for tonight." She cracked eggs into a bowl and whisked them with a fork. "We'll need to go into town for some supplies, unless you have an arrangement with a neighbor for milk and butter. It will make cooking easier."

He hung his jacket by the hat. "No arrangement with the neighbors. I sold my cow to the Hendersons after Ann left. There wasn't a need to keep her for one person. I do most of my eatin' in town."

She poured the eggs into the frying pan where the bacon drippings she'd found in a jar on a shelf above the stove sizzled. "I'll need milk for cooking." She cleared her throat, hating to ask for something else on a day when he'd done so much. "And for me to drink."

He nodded. "For the baby?"

"Yes."

"I'll buy a cow tomorrow."

Rena scooped the eggs onto plates and set them on the table. "It's ready. I'm sorry there isn't more to it."

Scott joined her at the table. "Don't apologize. It's more than I'd have made for myself tonight."

He sat opposite her and reached out a hand for prayer. Her father had always insisted that they hold hands while he blessed the food—even during the years she'd refused to attend services with him. This was different. Scott was a man of faith who practiced his beliefs in his home, but he was also her husband. Only in name, but still her husband.

Why then did she not want to reach across the table? She wouldn't explore the possibility that it was a matter of trust. Her father had been her protector. Could she grow to trust Scott in time?

Scott wasn't unfamiliar. He was often in her father's home. But they didn't interact more than the necessary pleasantries. She'd cooked the meals, and he'd sat across from her. The wide table had prevented them from holding hands while offering thanks for their food as he'd sat next to her father. The table here in his home was smaller. It was expected. And he waited.

She took a deep breath and dropped her hand into his. His grip was gentle, and his words sincere, as he offered thanks for their meal and for her efforts to prepare it. The next words stung her heart.

"And, Lord, please help us to make the best of this marriage. I know neither one of us saw it coming, but You take care of Your children. I'm asking You to take care of us. Amen."

He released her hand and reached for the platter of ham.

She slid her hand to her lap. Heat spilled into her cheeks. No one had ever prayed for her except Momma and Papa.

Scott passed the ham to her. "I guess we need to talk about how we're going to do this."

Rena nodded and took the platter from him.

"You saw Ann's room?" He pointed to the door in the front corner of the main room.

"I did. I took a few minutes to look around while you were in the barn." She spooned eggs onto her plate. Her appetite hadn't been much for the last few weeks. The baby needed her to eat, so she'd try again.

"I think it will serve you well. There's enough space for a cradle." He speared a bite of ham. "I hope you don't think me too familiar to speak of such things."

"No. There are things that must be done." She pushed the eggs around on her plate. "Though the need for a cradle will be months away from now."

"Can you tell me how long?" His lowered voice, and the fact that he kept his eyes on his plate let her know that he was possibly as uncomfortable with this topic as she was.

"The baby should arrive near the beginning of August."

He looked up then. "I'll get started on the cradle this month. I want to finish it before spring. There'll be planting and such to do then."

"I could see if Papa will buy one. It doesn't seem right for you to have to build it." It was her turn to look away. "I'm certain he'd be willing to buy the cow, too."

"I won't be needing any help taking care of you or the baby." Scott set his fork down. "I know we made this decision quickly today, but be assured I considered everything I could think of before we were married. A man doesn't let another man provide for his family."

She'd hurt his feelings. His pride. "I meant no disrespect."

He folded his napkin and slid his chair back. "None taken." He took his dishes to the cabinet against the side wall of the cabin. He poured the water she had heated on the stove into the basin and slid in his dishes.

Rena jumped to her feet when she saw his intent. "I'll do the dishes, Sheriff." She tried to elbow him from in front of the basin.

He looked down at her, and she realized how close they were. Standing here, side by side, in their home was too familiar. She backed away and ran her palms down the front of the apron she'd found on a peg near the stove.

"Please let me do the washing up." She wasn't one to beg. It went against her nature. Nor was she one to accept charity. If she didn't work, she'd feel like his actions toward her were borne of pity.

"Okay." Scott dropped the cloth into the sudsy water and stepped back from the cabinet. "Do you think you could call me Scott? If we're going to make this marriage appear real to the people in town, we're gonna have to practice being nice to one another."

"I'll try." She picked up the cloth and wiped the first dish. "There's an awful lot of new things to adjust to."

"We can do it. It'll take time, but we'll work it out." He went to the back door. "I'll bring in more wood while you do that. Then we can sit in front of the fire and finish our conversation."

He was out the door in a swift motion. She could hear him splitting logs while she cleaned the kitchen. It seemed they had one trait in common. They busied themselves with work when they were uncomfortable.

The circumstances of the day would have them both busy for weeks to come. She was sure of it.

Scott lifted the latch and pushed the door, using one foot to open it wide enough to enter with the double armload of wood. Rena was drying the last plate when he entered the cabin.

"I'm afraid we're in for a cold snap. The clouds gathering this evening look like they're full of rain." He leaned over the hearth and let the wood fall out of his arms. He added two logs to the fire and stacked the rest.

"I wish I'd thought to bring my quilts." She shivered and wrapped her arms around her middle.

He moved the rocking chair close to the fire. "Sit here and warm up. I'll find something for you to use tonight. We can go back to your father's house tomorrow and gather the rest of your things." He sat on the hearth and picked up a length of wood that he'd been whittling on for days. "Do you mind if I work while we talk?"

She shook her head. "No. I'll be bringing my sewing with me. It'll help to fill the evenings."

"Ann and I would sit and work after supper most nights." He held the wood up to the light of the fire and twisted it one way and another, deciding where to make his next cuts. "I miss her."

"You must. Being your only family and all." Rena set the rocker in motion. The hem of her dress puddled on the rug she'd beaten clean earlier. The toe of her shoe peeked out from beneath the fabric that swayed as she rocked.

"Martin Fleming is a good man. I knew when he and Ann met that I'd lose her to him." He cut away a stubborn knot from the wood and tossed it into the fire.

"They seemed very happy."

He agreed with a nod.

Silence fell in the room. She rocked, and he carved for several minutes. Then he saw her rub her arms again.

"I'll be right back." He put his wood on the hearth and his knife on the mantel. In his room, he opened the wardrobe and lifted the last sweater his mother had knitted for him. Underneath, he found the quilt she'd made when he was a boy. He tugged it out, returned the sweater to its place and closed the wardrobe.

Back in the main room, he laid the quilt on the hearth, careful to keep it away from sparks and ash. "I'll warm this, and you can use it tonight."

Rena stopped rocking and leaned close to inspect the quilt. "What a lovely pattern. Did Ann make it?"

"My mother did. Ann has one like it, but hers is pink and green. Our mother made them for us when we were children." He picked up the knife and wood and returned to his place in front of the fire.

She reached out a hand and caressed the blue and brown starburst that formed the center of the quilt. "Are you sure you want me to use it? What about you?"

"I have another." He didn't want to talk to her about his mother. The woman who'd given everything she had to care for him and his sister. She'd worked odd jobs, taken in laundry, baked for others and anything else to put food on their table after their father had died.

His mother was the perfect picture of everything a mother should be. He wasn't ready to share that with Rena. Not on the night he'd married her to give her child a name.

They were completely different women. His mother had been quiet and settled. Determined and strong.

Rena was almost never quiet and certainly not settled. Though he couldn't deny her bravery at marrying a man she'd always kept at a distance to protect her unborn child.

He wouldn't talk about his mother to her. Not now. Maybe not ever.

Scott put the wood aside and stood to pace behind the settee that separated the kitchen from the main part of the room. "So." He ran a nervous hand through his hair and stepped in front of her chair. "What do you think we should establish as a sort of ground rules for what's going on here."

She had to crane her neck to see him, so he dropped onto the front edge of the settee and leaned toward her.

"Do you mean things like how to address one another? How to comport ourselves in public? That sort of thing?"

"Yes. We'll have to appear friendly, or people won't believe the child is ours."

Her face turned pink. "Really, Sheriff, I don't think we have to verbalize every detail."

"Scott. You're going to have to call me by my name."

The color began to fade from her cheeks. "Scott." The word was soft and seemed to come with great effort.

He answered her in kind. "Rena." He rubbed his palms down the length of his thighs. He should not be sweating on a cold December night. "I promise to be respectful of you. Neither of us expected to be in this situation."

"Thank you." She avoided his gaze. "I'll try to be friendly toward you."

He chuckled. "You better be careful. If you start being too nice to me, people will start to think you don't dislike me anymore."

She jerked her head up. "Surely getting married will convince them otherwise." She looked away and made him wonder if she was trying to cover her true feelings. "I never actually disliked you."

"Really?" He leaned back. "Then why all those suppers where you didn't say anything to me? You passed the food and spoke to your father, but it was clear that you were avoiding me."

"*Standoffish* is probably the way I'd describe it. I guess I thought you dismissed me. That you didn't like me as a person. So I didn't want to waste my time or efforts by trying to build a friendship with you." She shrugged one shoulder and stared into the fire. "I never meant to be unkind."

"You were never unkind. But you weren't friendly."

"If you feel that way about me, why did you agree

to this marriage?" Her eyes were open, honest. She was seeking the truth.

"I needed help here. And your father was right. A scandal now could cost him his position as mayor."

"And you the job as sheriff? I heard that part of the conversation. Do you believe that? Could he be ousted as mayor because of what I've done?"

"People can be mean-spirited and unforgiving. It's not right, but it happens." He didn't want to add the weight of blame to her.

"That's so unfair."

"It is. But we can't worry about what might happen. We did the right thing, and now we move on. God isn't so much concerned with where we've been but where we are."

"And where are we?"

"We are at the beginning of an arrangement to benefit both of us, the child and your father. We need to make the best of it."

"But you agree that we aren't expecting more from me than someone to help you handle the chores here?"

"Yes. And you know that I'll take care of the needs of you and the baby, but I'm not wanting anything like a real marriage out of this. I wasn't looking for that with anyone. I don't expect it from you." Did she flinch? "I don't mean that in an unkind way."

"You're merely stating the obvious." She brushed her hands across her skirt and stood. "I think I'll turn in. It's been a long day, and there's a lot to do tomorrow, if we're going to get my things from town. I've got my work cut out for me here, too."

She picked up the quilt and hugged it close. "Thank you for all you did today. I am grateful. I hope you know that." The effort it took her to say the words was unmistakable.

He nodded. "I do."

She closed the door to Ann's room.

He leaned against the back of the settee with his arms crossed behind his head. *What have I gotten myself into?*

Lord, this didn't surprise You, but it has thrown me like a wild horse. Help me land without getting hurt. Or hurting anyone else.

The fire crackled and settled. He added several logs to it and headed for bed. He had a feeling that tomorrow wouldn't be the only long day in his future. He'd take them one at a time. Riding into Gran Colina with a new bride in the morning would be a challenge. Their sudden wedding would surely keep the town gossips busy for weeks to come. He hoped he and Rena could portray a convincing couple without making either of them uncomfortable.

Chapter Three

The smell of frying bacon woke Rena the next morning. Her stomach wrenched.

Please help me, Lord. How long is this going to go on? I don't have time to be sick all day, every day. I know I don't have a right to ask You for anything, but I'd sure appreciate a dose of mercy.

She slid her feet into her slippers and tied on her robe. She opened the door enough to see Scott at the stove with his back to her. She tiptoed across the floor of the main room and out the front door. The chilly air and damp ground were the only evidence of the rain she'd heard in the middle of the night. The sky was bright and clear.

A few minutes later, with one hand across her middle and the other holding her robe tight at the neck, she returned and hoped to make her way back to her room unnoticed.

"Oh, there you are." Scott was walking away from the door to her room. He pointed at the table but stumbled backward a couple of steps as he took in her appearance. "I, uh, breakfast is ready."

Rena made an effort to pull her robe tighter. She wasn't accustomed to being in a man's presence in such a state. There hadn't been time to brush her hair or make herself presentable before she'd taken ill. Shame covered her again. Scott continued his backward motion until he was on the opposite side of the room from her.

"Thank you. I'll be out in a few minutes." She dashed into her room and closed the door. Leaning against the cold wood, she vowed to avoid another instance of being caught in her nightclothes. Even if it meant she had to sleep in one of her dresses.

When she went back into the main room, Scott was taking his plate to the basin. "I thought we'd get an early start." He didn't look at her.

"That's fine. Is there anything you need me to do before we go? Gather the eggs? Feed the chickens?"

"Nope. It's all done." He was at the door, donning his hat. "Have your breakfast while I hitch up the wagon."

"I'll be quick." She watched him button his jacket. "But you're going to have to let me help. Tomorrow morning I'll follow you around and learn the chores."

He lifted the door latch. "We'll deal with tomorrow when it gets here." He was out the door before she could respond.

The first part of the ride to town was silent. It wouldn't do to arrive and face all the people they knew without having said a dozen words to each other.

"If you want to drop me off at my father's house, I can pack this morning while you work." She held her best reticule in her lap. The navy velvet fabric and black-trimmed bag felt fancy compared to her mood. She'd worn her Sunday best for the wedding. The reticule had completed her outfit, and she hadn't thought to pack another one in her valise.

"Do you have a trunk?" Scott kept his eyes on the road.

"My mother's. It should hold everything. I don't have much. My clothes and sewing." She bit her bottom lip. She wouldn't tell him about the items she'd hidden in the bottom of the trunk for years. Things she thought a bride would need when she married. A fancy frame for a wedding photograph. A lace runner for the dresser she'd hoped to have in the room she'd share with the husband she'd dreamed of as a girl.

Eugene had turned that dream into a nightmare. The fancy things she'd collected had lost the joy she'd known when she'd bought them.

She would still bring them, but there was nothing in that trunk to turn this marriage into a happy event. No trinket or keepsake could polish the tarnish off her circumstances. Today she was married, but her problems were far from over.

Scott's reply dragged her back to the moment at hand. "Good. I'll leave you to it then. When you finish, come to my office. We'll have lunch at the hotel before we go to the mercantile and purchase the things you'll need for the house. Or, if you'd rather, you can give me a list. I'll drop it off, and Mrs. Busby can gather everything up for you."

"That's probably for the best. It would save us time." She twisted her gloved hands together. "We don't have to go to lunch. I can make something at Papa's or after we get home."

He glanced at her. "What kind of husband would the folks of Gran Colina think me if I didn't treat you to a nice meal after our wedding? We didn't have time yesterday, but today they'll be expecting me to treat you."

"So you are thinking about how people are going to react to us."

"I am. And so should you be. You're going to have to talk to Charlotte. She's not the kind to let you up and get married without giving her all the details."

Rena gasped. "Oh no. I hadn't thought of that. Giddiness and giggles will be on her mind." She shook her head. "I won't be able to do that."

"I suggest you tell her that a married lady doesn't discuss the things of marriage with anyone other than her husband. She's mature enough to accept that."

"She's going to have questions. Lots of questions about when we started courting and why we didn't tell anyone."

"Hmm. It seems you're going to have to be the most convincing. Men aren't likely to ask me that sort of thing." He squinted against the morning sun. "Tell her I'm not the kind to talk about such things. That I'm real private about matters of the heart." He frowned.

Rena imagined there was more truth to his suggestion than he'd be willing to admit. After Louise's marriage to Thomas Freeman, he hadn't courted anyone that she knew of. Surely Louise's betrayal had wounded him. "Thank you. That's just the type of answer to keep her from pressing me."

Scott slowed the wagon to cross the railroad tracks and headed through the center of town. The stationmaster lifted a hand as they drove by. "Morning, Sheriff. Mrs. Braden. Must say I'm a bit surprised to see the two of you back in town so soon after your wedding."

Rena sensed Scott stiffen on the seat beside her. He nodded and answered, "Good morning."

"Oh my. I think we're going to be the object of more attention than I realized." She straightened her back and held on to the rail on the side of the seat.

"Yes. Not much more interesting has happened in town in recent weeks."

In the center of town, he steered the wagon to the right. One more left turn would find them at her father's house. The home where she'd grown up with her father and mother.

How she wished her mother had been here to advise her. Her death had left Rena and Papa with memories of a wonderful woman and no one to guide Rena through her years of becoming a young lady. If her mother had lived, she felt certain she wouldn't be in this situation. Momma would have known she was sneaking around with Eugene. Just like she'd known when Rena had broken the sugar bowl that had been in their family for two generations.

Momma had known so many things without being told. Could Rena ever hope to be that kind of mother? Doubt filled her again.

Scott stopped in front of the yellow clapboard house. He bounded to the ground and came to help her down. It was so uncomfortable. Living in town had meant she could walk almost everywhere she went. Climbing in and out of a wagon with a man's assistance was something she'd have to get used to. Knowing the man was her husband caused a peculiar feeling in the pit of her stomach.

"Do you want to come inside and speak to Papa?" She turned to walk through the front gate of the low picket fence that separated the small yard from the dirt street.

"I'll come in long enough for you to make your list."

They entered the house and found her father in his study. The large desk he sat behind was one of Rena's favorite pieces of furniture. She loved how Papa looked behind it. As a girl, she'd always thought him the most important man in town.

Knowing what he'd done yesterday to protect her reputation and the town's future proved she was right.

"Good morning, Scott." Papa rose to shake hands with Scott. He turned to Rena. "Hello, Rena." The way he lowered his tone when he greeted her told of his ongoing sadness.

The sting of her heart was fresh. Never had he been cool or reserved with her. How she hated the pain she'd brought to him. The fracture of their relationship was her fault. And she found it unbearable. He'd been so pleased when she'd started attending services with him again. How she hated the disappointment he must feel at realizing how desperate her need for God was.

"I've come to get my things."

Papa nodded but didn't speak.

Scott had his hat in his hand. "Oscar, I'd like to speak to you about a matter of town business if you have a few minutes."

"Certainly." Papa returned to his chair.

Rena looked at the two of them. Scott lowered his tall frame into a wooden chair opposite her father. They settled in for a conversation as they had done many times over the last couple of years. The likelihood of her being the topic of today's business was undeniable. "I'm going into the kitchen to make that list, Scott."

"Fine. I'll be here when you've finished." He didn't even turn to look at her. As she closed the door, he said, "I think there are some things we can do that will help—" The heavy door kept her from hearing anything else he said.

At the table in the kitchen, she made a list of all she could imagine she'd need for a week of cooking and cleaning. It took longer than she imagined. She racked her brain for things she remembered Scott commenting on that she'd cooked in the past. Those items went on the top of the list.

She was almost done when she heard the door to the study open.

"Thank you for taking care of that for me, Scott." Her father's voice carried down the long hallway and into the kitchen.

"You're welcome, sir. We're in this together. That's the only way for it to succeed."

Her father closed the study door. As she listened to Scott's boots on the wooden floor, she wished she hadn't caused them both so much work and worry.

Scott came into the kitchen. "Do you have the list?"

She stood and handed him the paper. "If it's too much, let me know. I can pare it down."

He read the list. A few lines down the page he smiled and gave an approving sound and a nod. "This is fine." He tucked the paper into the pocket of his pants. "Is there anything you need from me before I leave? Do I need to get the trunk out of the attic?"

"No. It's in my room."

"Okay. I'll be working then. You come when you're done."

"It won't take too long. I may try to see Charlotte if I finish before it's time to eat."

Scott nodded and left her to her work.

She pulled her apron from its hook by the back door and draped it over one arm. In the hall, she ran her hand along the edge of the frame on the table near the bottom of the stairs. It was her favorite photograph of her mother.

Everything was spinning around in her head. She was leaving this house today. Her best friend would be strained by a refusal to discuss her sudden marriage. That action could cause her to lose Charlotte's trust.

Was there no end to the consequences of one choice made months ago without thought for the future?

In the room she'd lived in all of her life, Rena opened her mother's trunk and put the apron inside. She opened the bureau drawers and took out the things that would make her new house a home. Tears trickled down her cheeks, and she dashed them away.

This was the only choice she'd had. Her baby required a home and father. Papa and Scott had made that happen. Rena wouldn't mourn that choice. There had been no other course of action.

Next she tucked the dresses that hung in her wardrobe into the trunk with care. She pressed the pillow from her bed on top of the dresses and lowered the lid of the chest. Her shoes were put in a crate that she lined with a length of fabric. She pulled the quilt from her bed and folded it.

Standing in the center of the room, she wondered if Papa would mind if she took the washstand. It had been her mother's. The blue flowers painted on the white basin and pitcher were as delicate as she remembered her mother to be.

A knock sounded on the bedroom door. She opened it to find her father.

"May I come in?"

"Of course." She stepped aside. "I was just finishing up here."

Papa looked around the room. "I'm not sure what I'll do with myself now that you're grown and married. I'll miss our talks after supper. And reading the Bible together at night." He turned to her. "It's done my heart good to read with you these last few weeks. Your momma would want you to have this." He put her mother's Bible in her hand. "Promise me you'll keep reading it."

"I will, Papa." Her breath caught. He might be upset with her, but his love was still there.

"And come see me. Come here or to my office when you're in town." His voice cracked a bit on the last words.

Rena flung herself into his arms. "Oh, Papa! I'm so sorry I've made a mess of things. Please forgive me." She sobbed against his chest.

"Hush, child. You're forgiven." He patted her back. "I know you've chosen a difficult path for your life, but God loves you. And so do I." He made soft sounds of comfort in her ear. "Perhaps in time, Scott will grow to love you, too. You must give him time."

"I don't see how he could ever want me for his wife. No man could." She sniffed and pulled a handkerchief from the pocket of her skirt as she backed away from him. "I don't think I'll ever be able to trust again. I feel so betrayed."

Her father tucked a loose strand of hair behind her ear. "He already took you as his wife, Rena. Be fair to him. He's done a great thing for our family. And he's a good man."

"I'll treat him with respect."

"That's a good place to start." He pulled his watch from his vest pocket. "I have a meeting in a few minutes. Is Scott coming back here now?"

"We're going to lunch before we come for my things."

"How nice for you." He gave a final perusal of the room.

"Papa, may I take the washstand with me?"

He turned to the corner of the room. "That was a gift from me to your mother on our first anniversary." He smiled. "I remember how pleased she was to be surprised." He nodded at her. "I think she would want you to have it."

"Thank you, Papa." She gave him another hug. "Not just for the gift, but for everything. You are a wise man. I am grateful for your help. Pray that I'll be able to live up to the demands of running a homestead and being a mother."

"I will." He left her standing there in the room that no longer felt like home.

Her things were ready to be taken away. The childhood she'd lived here was over, and a new life waited for her in the sheriff's office on the other side of town. It was time to go.

Scott couldn't concentrate. The words on the papers on his desk swam in front of him like ants crawling on a pie at a picnic.

Married. He was married.

And not for any reason he'd have chosen.

He shook his head and straightened the papers on his desk into small stacks. On top was a list he'd made during the course of the morning. Every time he thought of something he needed for the homestead or Rena, he jotted it on the small piece of paper.

A ring. Rena didn't have a wedding ring. He could

get her one soon. They hadn't discussed it. Perhaps it was something she didn't think she should ask about, but he knew giving her one was the right thing to do.

The tip of the pencil broke, and he pulled out his knife to sharpen it.

The door opened, and Cyrus Busby from the mercantile came in. "I got that order ready for you."

Scott pushed the knife blade across the pencil again and nicked his thumb. "Ouch!" He dropped the knife and put the pad of his thumb to his lips. With the other hand he added the ring to his list.

"Thanks, Cyrus. I appreciate that. We'll be by your place this afternoon to pick it up." He folded the list and put it in his pocket.

The door opened again, and Rena entered the office. "I've finished—" She stopped short when she saw Cyrus. "Oh, hello, Mr. Busby."

Cyrus nodded. "Mrs. Braden."

Rena's cheeks filled with pink at the words.

Scott didn't like seeing her uncomfortable. "Thanks again, Cyrus. We'll come by later."

Cyrus made a motion like he would leave, but he stopped with his hand on the door. "You know, I never noticed the two of you showing much interest in one another. Don't seem like you were even courting, and now you're married."

Scott moved from behind his desk and came to stand beside Rena. He put his arm around her shoulders and felt her stiffen at his touch. A glance at her face showed her determination to protect their privacy.

He spoke to the mercantile owner. "Sometimes these notions come on a man sudden like."

Cyrus rubbed a hand across the stubble on the side of his round face. "Sudden like, huh?"

"Yes." Scott wanted to laugh at the man's puzzled expression, but that would ruin the effect. "If you'll excuse us, I promised my wife lunch over at the hotel."

"Sure." Cyrus went out the door slowly.

Rena stepped away from Scott as soon as Cyrus left. "Was that necessary?"

Scott chuckled. "I have probably just made short work of an explanation to the townsfolk for our sudden marriage." He pushed his hat on and opened the door for her. "With Cyrus's need to know and share everything he learns about anyone's business, I dare say most of Gran Colina will be talking about our whirlwind romance over their evening meals tonight."

"Oh, I see." The sadness that had shrouded her features at the homestead lifted just a bit. "You are right. I only hope Charlotte is as easy to convince. I just finished packing my things and haven't had a chance to see her yet."

"I imagine she'll be in the restaurant when we go. You can tell her then."

At Green's Grand Hotel, Charlotte was indeed working. She showed them to a table by the window and promised to return for a chat as soon as she'd helped to serve the lunch crowd.

Rena ate the special with more enthusiasm than he'd seen from her in the last two days.

"Are dumplings a favorite of yours?" He cut into his steak and took a bite.

She dabbed the corners of her mouth with a fancy napkin. "Yes. Charlotte's mother is an amazing cook."

He lowered his voice. "I'm glad to see your appetite restored."

"Don't worry about me. I'll be fine."

"Did you have an opportunity to speak with your father?"

"Yes. We had a good talk."

She cleared her throat, so he decided to change the subject. "I want to stop at the livery and see if Russell Henderson knows anyone who has a cow for sale."

Rena buttered a slice of bread. "Are you certain you won't let me ask Papa about that? I'm sure he'd be glad to help with the expenses you'll be burdened with on my account. You could think of it like a dowry of sorts."

"I will provide what we need. You know me well enough to know that I speak my mind." He lifted his glass of tea. "And that I rarely change it once I've made it up."

"I do."

Charlotte came to the table. "It's been so busy today." She rested a hand on Rena's shoulder. "But I have time for you to tell me all about how you managed to get married without any clue of your courtship to me—your dearest friend in the world." Charlotte put both hands just below her throat and pressed. "Why, I may never get over the hurt." Her wink at Rena revealed her teasing nature.

"Charlotte!" Mrs. Green's voice came from the open kitchen door. "I need your help."

"Oh well. Maybe I'll get a minute soon. Enjoy your lunch." Charlotte waved her fingers and rushed to help her mother.

"Seems as though Charlotte isn't opposed to our arrangement."

Rena folded her napkin and took a drink of her tea. "It's not in her nature to think poorly of anyone. She always looks for the best and believes it. Sometimes even after she's learned otherwise."

The next few minutes seemed like an hour. He ate his steak, but it wasn't as satisfying as the last time he'd eaten at the hotel. No doubt, his appetite was as affected as Rena's had been by the changes in their lives. But he wasn't about to leave a good steak on the plate, even if she did sit in silence with her mind on unknown thoughts.

Charlotte came back to the table as he finished his meal. She carried two small plates and put them on the table in a flourish. "Tea cakes. Mother sends her blessings and congratulations on your marriage. She also apologizes for being so busy. She'll try to stop by your table if she can."

A smile crossed Rena's face. "How very kind. Thank her for me."

"I will." Charlotte indicated an empty chair. "May I?"

"Certainly."

Charlotte sat and rested her elbows on the table.

"Tell me everything." Her wide eyes made Scott know he didn't want to be at the table for this conversation.

"Rena, I'm going back to the office. You enjoy your visit with Charlotte." He pushed his chair back and stood.

"Please don't leave on my account," Charlotte said.

"You ladies have your talk. I've got work to do." He dropped a hand on Rena's shoulder. "Come to my office when you're done." Again he felt her tense at his touch. He hated to add to her discomfort, but he didn't intend his wife to be the subject of gossip when her pregnancy became obvious. It was best he show her the kind of attention a husband would be expected to show to prevent undue attention from others later.

He pulled money from his pocket and gave it to Rena. "Settle the bill for us, please." He picked up a tea cake and took a bite. He lifted it in salute to thank Charlotte and headed for the door.

He had his hand on the door when Charlotte's father called to him.

"Sheriff, can I trouble you for a minute?"

Scott ate the rest of his cookie as he walked to the registration desk. "Afternoon, Charles. What can I do for you?"

"Well, I hate to say anything, but I think I should, seeing how close my Charlotte is to your wife. And her being the mayor's daughter and all."

The hair stood up on the back of Scott's neck. Had their plan already been discovered? "If you have knowledge of something I need to know, I'd be grateful if you'd share." He kept his voice calm but braced himself for what might be coming next.

"I was in the post office a few minutes ago. Cyrus Busby was in there, too. He was asking Miss Alexander if she'd had any inkling of your romancing Miss Livingston before yesterday."

He'd have to answer carefully. It was one thing for Cyrus to spread the news that they had a whirlwind romance. It was another thing entirely for him to question whether there was a romance. "He asked me the same thing in my office just before lunch. You know he's always looking for something to talk about."

Charles chuckled. "Like a woman on a wagon train."

Scott laughed. "I told him our relationship was sudden. You know how we men are. Once we make up our mind about a thing, there's no need to dally over it."

"That's true. Just the same, I think you should know what was said." Charles looked around and lowered his voice. "Miss Alexander said that Jack Jefferson asked her about the two of you this morning. He seemed to be hinting that there was some unknown reason for your sudden nuptials. He told her that one day he'd prove to Gran Colina that you and the mayor weren't the best leaders for our town. He said to watch what happened in the election. She didn't like the sound of it and told Cyrus as much."

"Jack Jefferson has been on the hunt for a reason to discredit me since I took his nephew's job. Never mind that Gilbert never lifted a hand to slow the tide of crime in Gran Colina." Scott didn't like the sound of this gossip. Not one bit. "Thanks for letting me know. I suggest you ignore Jefferson. Just like I have to on almost everything."

Charles nodded. "Thanks for bringing your missus here for lunch. I expect we won't be seeing as much of you now that you'll have someone at home to cook for you."

"Rena is a fine cook, that's for sure and certain." He slapped the counter with his palm. "I'll try to stop in for lunch sometimes."

As he stepped onto the sidewalk, he noticed Jack Jefferson coming out of the bank with Thomas Freeman. The two men were often together. Jefferson owned the largest ranch in the county. He was probably the biggest depositor at Freeman's bank.

When Jefferson saw Scott, his usual sneer became a twisted grin. Nothing Jack Jefferson wanted for Gran Colina was good for the town. And he seemed determined to fight Scott and the mayor at every turn.

Scott would pray for the man again tonight. Prayer was the thing that kept him from allowing anger to build up inside and turn him to the same kind of bitter person that Jack Jefferson had become. Prayer had brought him through his broken engagement to Louise. He knew it would bring him through the coming election and help him to build a solid, if not loving, marriage with Rena.

His personal values made Scott want to live a good life, but now he must take extra care to remain above reproach. Or marrying Rena would only serve to provide him with a cook and a housekeeper. Something he wouldn't need if Jefferson found out the truth and used it to destroy Rena's reputation, ultimately costing him and the mayor their jobs.

With the election set for April, whatever Jack Jefferson had planned would soon come to light.

Chapter Four

Rena picked up a tea cake. "I love these. I wish your mother would share the recipe."

Charlotte laughed. "You know how she guards her recipes. She's only shared them with me because she needs my help in the kitchen. I had to promise never to breathe a word of any of the ingredients before she would let me see her recipe box."

"They are delicious." Rena finished off the tea cake, but she knew Charlotte would not be hindered in her pursuit of the story of how Rena and Scott came to be together.

"You have to tell me all about how you got married." Charlotte leaned forward in her chair. "I can't believe you kept this from me for so long. Or was it that long?" Her eyebrows lifted in a teasing fashion.

"I will tell you that it was very sudden, but Scott is private about these things. He wouldn't be comfortable with me talking about it."

"But I'm your best friend, and you used to tell me

everything." Charlotte's lighthearted voice let Rena know she wouldn't push for answers.

"You are a dear friend, Charlotte."

Charlotte leaned close and lowered her voice. "You won't tell me just a little bit?"

Rena shook her head. "I guess it's part of growing up. There comes a time when there are things you just can't share." She smiled and patted her friend's hand. "I've learned that over the last few months."

"Promise me this won't be the end of our sharing."

"Of course not, we'll always be close."

"I am very happy for you." She looked around the room and back at Rena. "But I must confess that I'm jealous. In a good way. My mother will never let me court anyone who catches my fancy."

Rena loved her friend and hoped that she would never know the depth of pain Rena had endured over the last two months. "Your mother is only protecting you. Remember the time you thought you were in love with Nathan Taylor? You thought he was so handsome." They both dissolved into giggles.

Charlotte tried to catch her breath. "I can't believe that boy put a frog on my head, and then thought I'd want to eat my lunch with him."

"And you had to endure his teasing until the day he moved away."

"Five years later! I've never been happier to see someone leave town. But I was right about one thing. He was handsome." Charlotte grew serious. "You're right though. Momma was looking out for me. She still does."

"You are blessed to have a mother who loves you so."

The agreement on Charlotte's face was sincere. "You're right." She giggled. "My pa could've married a mean old lady after my mother died. I'm so glad he married Momma instead."

"God will bring you the right person in His time. Be patient and prayerful. I promise you'll never be sorry if you wait on the person God has for you." If only someone had given her that advice. In truth, Rena knew her stubbornness would have prevented her from listening. How she wished she had never met Eugene Rodgers.

The smile on Charlotte's face let Rena know that her friend had no inkling of the true situation Rena was in. "Well, I hope He doesn't wait too long. I'm three months older than you, and you're already married."

Rena spent a few more minutes with her friend, and then made her way to Scott's office. When she climbed the steps, she could hear Jack Jefferson's raised voice carrying through the closed door.

"I don't know what's going on here, Braden, but I'll get to the bottom of it. You act all high-and-mighty, but this town was better off before the likes of you came."

Rena reached for the door, but it flew open, and Jack Jefferson stormed out. She stumbled backward.

Scott was right behind the man and caught her elbows in his strong hands. He helped her gain her balance. "Are you hurt?"

"No, just startled." Rena took a step away from him. He was too close.

"Jefferson, you'd be wise to calm down and take

care. I won't let you bring harm to my wife or anyone else in this town."

Jack Jefferson's only acknowledgment of his words was a raised hand flung outward in indifference.

"I heard him as I came up the steps." Rena stared after the man. She lowered her voice. "Was he here because of me?"

"You know Jefferson well enough to know that he doesn't need a reason for anything he does. He's motivated by the anger that rules his heart."

She lowered her gaze to his boots. They needed a good brushing, and his pants could do with a good laundering. She had a lot of work to do. "I'm sorry."

"It's not your fault." He pushed open the door to the office and held it for her to enter. "Will you come sit by the stove and let me finish some work? I won't be long."

Rena sat in a chair on the opposite side of his desk and looked around at the worn furnishings while he made notes in a journal. The two cells on the back wall were empty. The afternoon light spilled into the room through the small barred windows on the back wall.

"Is there anything I can do for you?"

He shook his head and held up one finger but did not look up from his work. The pencil in his hand flew across the page in short, deliberate strokes. At the end of the page, he made a forceful dot and swirled the tip of the pencil in a quick signature. "All done." He closed the journal and locked it in the drawer of his desk. "Let's go by the livery and get your cow." He grabbed his hat from the peg near the front window and pushed it onto his head. "I stopped in earlier and Henderson had one for sale."

"That's welcome news." Rena stepped onto the porch and waited while he locked the door. "Is there anything else we need to do while we're in town?"

"No. We can pick up your trunk first, and then we'll get the cow on our way out of town."

The afternoon sun was deep in the sky when they turned down the lane toward their cabin. Everything she would bring from her past into her future was in the trunk that sat in the bed of the wagon. Scott had removed the cow's bell and tied her so she'd follow along behind them.

"How are you feeling?" Scott glanced at her as she looked behind them to check on the cow.

"Tired. It's been another long day." She didn't want to complain, but the fatigue was like none she'd ever known.

He pulled the wagon in front of the porch and set the brake. She moved to the edge of the seat. "Wait, and I'll help you down."

"Thank you." She put her hand in his and stepped cautiously out of the wagon. "I'll figure out a way to do that by myself soon."

"No need." He picked up the cowbell and reattached it to the cow's harness. "If you don't mind, I'll take care of the animals and bring your trunk in later."

"I'll come along, and you can teach me to milk her."

He untied the cow from the wagon and stood holding the end of the rope. He studied her with his head tilted to one side. "Okay. You might want to change your clothes first."

She looked down at her cream-colored coat. "My other clothes are in the trunk."

Scott chuckled. "Let me get this girl settled in the barn, and I'll drag your trunk into the cabin."

"Thank you." Rena went into her new home and tugged off her coat and gloves. She laid them across her bed and removed her hat.

She went to stand in front of the mirror that must have been Ann's. "The learning of new ways starts now, ma'am." She smoothed the front of her skirt. Her palms stopped in her middle, and her thoughts turned to the child growing inside her. "God, help me. There's so much to learn."

The sound of her trunk scrubbing across the porch caught her attention. She hurried into the front room and opened the door. She turned the rug at her feet sideways.

"If you can drag it onto the rug, it should slide across the floor easier."

Scott dragged the trunk onto the rug and dropped the end he carried with a thud. He straightened and brushed his hands together. "Good idea. I'd forgotten how strong a man has to be to move a woman's things."

"At least you had help when Ann moved out. I'm sorry I can't help you." She hated that he had to do everything himself.

He looked at her. "You don't need to feel like that. I've known you for a while. I know you're not shy of work and that you're hindered by your—" he hesitated "—circumstances."

"Thank you for saying that." She stepped out of his way. "If you can get that into my room, I'll change quickly and meet you in the barn."

She hadn't grown accustomed to acknowledging her pregnancy to herself, so it was awkward to hear him speak of her condition. An appreciation for his concern bored a hole in the wall around her heart.

Scott had unhitched the team and fed them. He was in front of the barn, washing the milk bucket when Rena came out of the cabin. She was a beautiful young woman, but the deep sadness in her soul was unveiled when they were alone.

Lord, please help her. I don't know the best way to help her, but I'll do what I can.

"You don't have to learn this tonight. You can start supper, and I'll bring in the milk." He turned the bucket upside down and shook out the rinse water.

She was tying her hair in a ribbon as she walked across the yard. "The more I learn now the better off I'll be."

"Okay. Do you want me to show you how first, or do you want to get right to it and learn on your own?"

Rena followed him into the barn, and they stood in front of the cow's stall. She squared her shoulders. "That depends. Are you a good teacher?"

He added hay to the trough, and the cow began to eat. "Can't say as I've had much experience teaching someone to milk a cow." He chuckled at the thought.

"Are you suggesting that if you have trouble learning it will be because of my way of teaching?"

"You tell me what to do." She walked beside the cow and patted her side. "Good girl. You be a good girl, and I'll be gentle." She kept one hand on the cow while she pulled the milking stool closer with the toe of her shoe. Then she lowered herself to the stool. "Okay, girl." She rubbed her hands together to warm them and reached out to milk the cow.

"It doesn't look to me like you need a teacher."

"I remember reading a storybook in school. The little boy in the story tried to milk the cow with cold hands and was very sorry."

"Then I think you're a better student than I would be a teacher." He was about to leave her to her task, when the cow bellowed.

"Whoa, girl." Rena's soft voice held a soothing quality. "I'm sorry." She rubbed her hands together again and, this time, succeeded in getting milk into the bucket.

"I'll leave you to your work." He backed out of the stall and went to feed the other animals.

A few minutes later, he saw her carrying the bucket toward the cabin. He smiled and shook his head. If she was that determined in everything she faced, she'd have no problems adjusting to life on a homestead.

A breeze swirled between where he stood at the gate of the corral and the cabin. It lifted the ribbon that held Rena's hair in place and tossed it across her face. She pulled it back with her free hand and kept moving. Even while lugging a bucket of fresh milk she looked calm and in control. He knew it wasn't true. Nothing in the last two days had happened the way either of them had planned. He knew in his heart that she'd never have married him for any other reason.

He remembered his mother's love for him. How she'd taught him to milk a cow and brush a horse. He'd learned so much from her. Things that got him through every day of his life as an adult.

Things Rena had never had to do. She'd surprised him with how well she'd handled the cow, but if she was going to survive on this homestead, she'd need other lessons. He knew his mother would want him to teach her.

Scott pulled the barn door closed and headed for the cabin. It probably wouldn't happen quickly, but he'd start tonight.

He unloaded the wagon and carried their supplies into the cabin while Rena cooked.

"Where do you want this?" He carried the stand for her bowl and pitcher.

She looked up from the pot of beans she stirred. "I'd like it in the corner by the window if it will fit."

"Okay." He pushed the door of her room open with his boot. "Over here?" He called over his shoulder and was startled when she spoke from right behind him.

"There." She pointed to her preferred spot. "And could you push the trunk a little bit to the right?"

He put the stand where she directed, and then shoved the trunk over. "Anything else?"

"Well, since you asked, could you move the bed to

that wall?" She looked a little sheepish. "The morning sun warms that part of the room."

"It does?" He nodded and pulled the bed frame to its new location.

"That's perfect." She looked around the room, and her gaze stopped on the trunk.

His sister had rearranged the furniture in the front room several times before she'd decided the first way he'd set it was the best. Pulling heavy things from one side of the room to another wasn't new to him. "What is it?" He followed her eyes. "Oh, now the trunk needs to be where the bed was before?"

Her mouth dropped open. "Yes! How did you know?" She scooted out of his way. "And the mirror should be over here."

He straightened from moving the trunk and made a show of sniffing the air. "Are the beans sticking in the pot?"

"Oh no!" She dashed by him on her way to the stove. "I completely forgot about supper."

Scott laughed and moved the mirror.

When he went back into the front room, she was pouring the beans into a bowl. "Only the ones on the bottom were scorched." She filled two cups with fresh milk and set them on the table.

"You did well with the cow." He sat on the hearth and tugged off his boots.

"Thank you." She put a plate of fried sausage on the table. "I know everything won't be as easy to conquer as that was, but I'm glad to be making progress."

"Have you ever lit a fire?"

Her back was to him as she pulled plates from the shelf on the far wall. "Papa always lit the fires at home." She turned to look at him over her shoulder. "He said it was man's work."

"He did, did he?" Scott was glad she had moments where she relaxed enough to tease him. She had often teased her father when Scott had occasion to be in their home. He'd enjoyed watching their easy relationship, even though she'd never made any effort to build a friendship with him.

"Said he'd never let Momma light a fire. Didn't want her to get the soot on her clothes."

"Is that so?" He chuckled and pulled a match from the cast-iron holder on the wall by the fireplace. "Well, your mother didn't live out on a homestead. Town ladies have a different kind of life."

She put the plates on the table. "What are you saying?"

"I'm saying that you've got a lot to learn about homesteading, and I think we need to start with the basics. You're good with a stove, but during the winter the fireplace will need to be kept lit while we're home. You'll be here during the day while I'm in town taking care of my work as sheriff."

"You could light the fire in the morning before you go." She stood on the far side of the table.

"And what if some night I'm kept in town on business? You could wake in the morning to find the fire out. Can't have you and the little one freezing in the cabin while I'm all cozy in my office with a fire in the stove."

"You mean to leave me here alone with a new baby and stay out overnight?" When had their light banter turned to fear in her?

He took a step toward her. "No, Rena. I was only teasing you with the possibility that I might be caught away overnight. I'm sorry. I didn't mean to frighten you."

She rubbed her hands up and down her arms as if she was cold. "I'm not frightened."

"Rena, I truly am sorry that the thought of being here alone isn't the same as the safety you felt in town in your pa's house." Scott looked at her. "Life on a homestead isn't like living in town. You're going to need to learn to tend the fire. I'll teach you to shoot, so you can protect yourself and the little one." He didn't mean to do it, but his eyes dropped to her midsection. "I'll pray you never need to shoot anyone or anything. But it is important for you to know how."

She shuddered, and he came to stand in front of her. "Don't worry. You're a brave person." Before he thought about what he was doing, he pulled her into his arms and held her against his chest. "You'll conquer the skills you need in no time."

Rena relaxed against him for a moment, and then bolted out of his embrace. "I'm not going to worry." She must have been dredged up the resolve in her eyes from the depths of her soul. It hadn't been there when he'd reached out to comfort her. She plucked the match from his hand and went to the fireplace. In no time at all the flames began to lick up the kindling. She tossed the match into the fire and spun around.

"Don't think that my life in town kept me from basic skills. I may have been a bit pampered as the mayor's daughter, but I'm an independent woman who can take care of herself, too." She lifted her cute nose up in the air just a fraction and grinned. She was trying to make him laugh and not focus on the fear she had shown.

He made a sweeping gesture and bowed in her direction. "I will remember your ability the next time I'm tempted to help you."

Her eyes narrowed almost imperceptibly at his poor choice of words. He hoped she didn't think he regretted helping her—or that he wouldn't want to help her in the future.

"Good." She crossed to the table. "Let's eat before these burned beans get cold."

Scott followed her lead and kept the conversation on easy matters for the rest of the evening. Only when he plumped up his pillow and settled into bed did he allow himself to think about her reaction.

Their lighthearted banter had been pleasant. He'd even enjoyed it. More than he'd thought he might. But in an instant Rena had become vulnerable. Her usual flighty and fun personality had been swallowed up in her pregnancy and abandonment.

Eugene Rodgers had stolen a lot from Rena last fall. Scott knew he couldn't restore her to the happy and carefree young lady she'd been before, but he was beginning to hope he could at least alleviate some of her pain.

Chapter Five

A warm glow on the horizon promised a beautiful sunrise when Rena looked through her bedroom window the next morning. She turned to the mirror in its new location in the corner of the room. Her sturdy skirt and blouse were just right for gathering eggs and feeding chickens. She tied her hair in a length of ribbon and went into the front room.

Scott stood at the stove and poured a cup of coffee. "Would you like a cup?"

She nodded. "How are you awake before me?"

A crowing sounded in the yard. "That rooster has been waking me up every day since Ann brought him home. He seems to hate me."

She accepted the coffee he offered. "Thank you. I have a feeling that rooster doesn't have anything to do with it. You probably woke him."

"Not the rooster." Scott handed her a plate loaded with eggs and toast. "I woke the chickens. I'm an early riser. It's the only way I can get all my work done." He joined her at the table.

Rena waited while he blessed their food and then added honey to her toast. "I'm ready for you to teach me the things I can do to help with the workload."

"You can milk the cow again." His dark navy shirt made the blue in his eyes stand out. The scruff on his chin was darker than usual. He probably hadn't had time to shave since the wedding.

The wedding. Had it only been two days earlier? How were they holding casual conversations about chores and animals when they were newly married? There was something very sad about the realization that she'd never know the joy of the first days of a marriage of true love. She must not think about his blue eyes and love. "We need to name the cow."

He picked up his coffee. "The cow's name is Bertie."

"Bertie?" She nodded. "It suits her."

"Henderson told me she belonged to a family who left last week to head back East. Life here was too much for the wife. They sold their cattle to Jack Jefferson and let their milk cow and horses go for a low price to the livery. Told Henderson to sell them and use the money to pay for their feed."

"How sad to give up their hope of a new life and have to parcel it out to others on their way out of town." She pondered her new life. It wouldn't be easy, but she was committed to it.

Lord, give me strength. I'm sure there are hard times ahead that I haven't considered. Help me not to fail you or my child again.

"It is, but they had somewhere to go. Somewhere

they wanted to be." He stared out the window as he spoke. "That counts for something." With those words, he scraped his chair backward and picked up his empty plate.

"Put that in the basin, and I'll wash up after the morning chores." Rena scooped the last bit of eggs onto her fork.

"Come to the barn when you finish. We'll start there."

The morning was full of new things. First she learned what feed was for which animals and how often they ate. Then Scott showed her how to move the horses and cow into the corral for the day. They hauled water from the well to the troughs in the corral, the pig pen and the hen house. The cool morning warmed as the sun climbed in the winter sky.

"I know I insisted that you teach me how to care for all the animals, in case I ever have to do the morning chores alone, but—" Rena wiped her forehead with her sleeve "—what would you say to sharing some of the water we're hauling for the animals with the homesteaders?"

He laughed. "There's a dipper hanging on the well."

She drank deeply and sank onto a bench near the corral fence. Scott drank two dippers of the cool water and sat beside her. He lifted his hat and wiped his face with a kerchief.

"That makes for a busy morning." The amount of work they'd done surprised her. Every day the same list of chores needed to be done. Rain or shine.

"You get used to it." He leaned against the fence post behind him.

"How did you manage on your own?"

He cut his eyes in her direction. "By neglecting the house."

"Ahh...now I understand." She smiled.

Scott looked across the yard at the cabin. "I hope you won't wear yourself out trying to clean it up."

"Don't worry." She pushed herself up from her resting spot. Sitting too near him made her uncomfortable. They needed to work side by side, but she knew he only allowed her presence for the sake of her father and his homestead. "I can handle it. It will be easier than feeding those pigs was."

"They're not so bad once you get to know them." He smiled and put on his hat. "They did seem to like you."

"If I have to pick a favorite, I'd say Bertie is it right now. At least she was patient with me."

Scott stood and stretched his back. "I'm going to ride into town for a while. Sometimes on Saturday it's late when I return. It all depends on who gets off the train and what happens at the saloon."

"Let me make you some lunch before you go."

"I'll stop in at the hotel and get a sandwich."

Rena liked the idea of a few hours on her own, but she wasn't sure how she'd feel in the late-night hours if he wasn't home. "Okay. Is there anything I should do if you are not back by sunset?"

"You could take care of the animals like we talked about this morning. The horses and Bertie will need to be put in their stalls." A serious expression crossed his face. "I'll try to be home before then. You haven't spent enough time out here to be left alone just yet."

"I know you have responsibilities. This is part of it. I'll be fine."

"I'm sure you will be. All the same, I'll be back."

Three hours later, Rena had scoured the kitchen area and table. The windows in the main room gleamed as the afternoon sun shone through and warmed the wooden floor. She opened the back door and stepped onto the porch that ran the length of the house. She hung the mop on the line between the posts that supported the roof and tossed the dirty water out of the bucket she'd found earlier.

She couldn't remember the last time she'd been so filthy. What she needed was a nice hot bath. A thorough search turned up a large washtub. It wasn't ideal, but with no alternative, she dragged it into her room while water heated on the stove.

In a short time, she had washed her hair, bathed and put on a clean dress. She sat in a rocking chair in front of the fireplace combing her hair dry. The rich aroma of the beef stew that simmered in a cast-iron pot on the stove filled the room. She leaned her head back and closed her eyes while she waited for the bread rising in a bowl on the table to be ready for the oven.

Rena awoke with a start at the sound of Scott's voice.

"Hey." She opened her eyes to see him squatted beside her chair. "Rough day?"

The cabin was almost dark and a glance toward the window revealed the last hints of daylight were fading.

"I didn't mean to fall asleep." She sat up and jerked around to see the pot of stew on the table. "Oh, good. You saved the stew."

"The bread is in the oven." He stood and added several logs to the dwindling fire in the fireplace. "I tried not to wake you, but supper is almost ready."

"I'm sorry. Let me see to the animals. You go ahead and eat. I won't be long."

"The evening chores are done. I got home about an hour ago."

"I didn't expect you so soon." She went to the cabinet and began to lay the table. "I only closed my eyes for a moment. I'm so fatigued."

Scott sat on the hearth and took off his boots. "You haven't had any time to rest in the last few days."

"You've had a long week yourself."

"Tomorrow is the Lord's day. I try to spend the afternoon in quiet. We can both use it after the week we've had."

She pulled the bread from the oven and turned it out onto the cutting board. "I'll have this sliced and ready in a minute. Thank you for all you did while I rested." She had promised to be a help to him. Sleeping while he worked was not in keeping with that promise.

"I'm used to doing all the chores myself. And the smell of this dinner lets me know I'll be the one laid back with my eyes closed soon. I haven't had cooking like this since Ann left."

Scott smiled at her when she took her seat opposite him. He thanked the Lord for the food and ate the hearty meal with gusto.

They'd made it through the third day. A day spent mostly in each other's company while they sorted through the workings of their new life together.

It wasn't so bad. Not really.

No sooner had the thought crossed her mind than her body sent her fleeing from the room.

Lord, this baby does not seem to be happy with me. Please calm the sickness in my body. And help me be the helper Scott deserves.

Scott waited at the table until Rena returned. He'd seen the signs of sickness in a woman with child before. It was hard to sit idly by, but he knew there was nothing he could do for her. He also knew she wouldn't thank him for attention she didn't want.

She sat down again and sipped water from her glass.

He cleared his throat. "So, what do you think about the homestead?"

Her shoulders slumped in apparent relief that he chose to ignore her sudden departure and return. "There is a lot of potential here. What are your plans for the place? I know you staked your claim not long after you came. Seems like you've made a lot of progress in that time."

He was proud of all he had accomplished, and her acknowledgment of his effort boosted his spirits a bit. "I hope to get a few head of cattle in the spring. I've run enough fence line to handle a small herd. I'll have to expand the fence quickly to keep up with the growth of the stock. We'll have a good garden, too. Do you think you can help to tend that?"

"Of course." She pushed the food around on her plate. "You may have to teach me though. Papa bought our food stores in town."

"It's not difficult. You just have to learn the difference between the plants and the weeds."

"So you want to raise cattle." She looked up from her plate. "Are you intending to compete with Jack Jefferson?"

The sound of the man's name made his jaw tighten. "No. I intend to provide for my family."

She stiffened. "I'm sorry, Scott. I wasn't implying anything ugly. It's just that I always think of the Jefferson Ranch when someone says they're going to raise cattle. He seems to have a hold on the ranching in the area."

"He may have the biggest ranch in the area, but he has no hold on me. Not for anything. The man is trying to take away my position as sheriff. His name was last thing I want to hear from my wife."

His wife. Rena was his wife. He looked up and saw the top of her head as she toyed with the food on her plate. His reaction was too forceful. It wasn't her fault Jefferson got under his skin. "You don't have to eat it, Rena. If you don't feel well, you don't feel well."

Her fork rattled as she dropped it onto her plate. "Please don't be cross with me. I'm sorry for upsetting you."

"I'm the one who should be apologizing. Not you. Forgive me. I should be more considerate of your condition." He reached across the table and covered her hand with his. "The stress of the last few days are wearing on me."

"That's my fault." Her words were barely more than a whisper.

"What do you say we agree that the whole thing is Jefferson's fault?" He squeezed her hand, and she smiled.

"Sure." She tugged her hand from beneath his and slid it into her lap. "I'd rather do that than quarrel with you."

He was ashamed. He'd taken her on as his wife to make her life better not worse. "I've got to take care of something in the barn. Will you leave a lantern on the table for me?" He pushed his chair away from the table and stood. He had to get outside. The space in the cabin seemed to shrink when they talked. Hurting her feelings made him feel guilty. It was a feeling he didn't like. "I won't be long, but I imagine you want to get to bed."

She pulled her lips inward and nodded. "I think that's best."

He shrugged into his jacket and left her gathering the dishes to wash.

Outside, a cool breeze ruffled the hair on the back of his neck. He pulled up his collar and walked to the corral. The night was dark with barely a sliver of moonlight.

A half hour in prayer didn't lift his burden. Rena was his responsibility now, but he didn't know how to be a husband. His father had died when he was a boy.

He sure didn't know how to take care of a woman who didn't want to be married to him.

Scott heard the door of the cabin open and close. He knew she was coming to check on him, but he didn't move from where he leaned on the corral fence.

"Scott, it's getting too cold to be out here. Please come inside." She didn't come close.

"I'll be in soon."

"You're only out here because of me." She stepped closer in the darkness. "That's not right. If you can't bear to be around me, I'll go to my room, but please come in out of the cold."

Come in out of the cold. He'd been living in the cold for ages. The cold that settled over his heart when Louise left him.

Rena took another step and now was beside him, facing the wintery darkness. "I won't be able to rest if you stay out here." She gave him a gentle nudge with her elbow. "You told me I need my rest."

This was more like the young woman he'd watched enjoy playful conversations with her father and friends. "Okay, but only if we can have something warm to drink before bed." He shivered and turned toward the house. "What about milk? I can heat it up for us." He tucked his hand inside her elbow and pivoted her to face the house.

"That sounds perfect." She let him lead her into the house and close the door behind them.

He threw the bolt to lock the door and shut out the night. Could he shut out the cold that covered his soul? Did he want to? If his heart thawed, the pain he'd suffered could return with a vengeance. That was a distraction he wouldn't risk while the future of Gran Colina was at stake.

Rena straightened her hat as she and Scott rode onto the churchyard the next morning. They were a few minutes late because he'd overslept. He'd been summoned into town in the middle of the night. Fighting at the saloon was a regular occurrence on Saturday nights. His deputy had sent for him because this particular fight had escalated to bloodshed. One man was in the jail, and the other was at Doc Taylor's office. His fate was still unknown when Scott had returned in the early morning hours.

The sounds of singing emanated from the sanctuary as Scott pulled the reins and stopped the wagon. "We don't have to do this. Not today." He turned to look at her. "No one would fault us for missing the first service after our wedding."

"We're already here. We may as well face the music."

"I hope that's not a reference to the piano playing of our dear preacher's wife." He laughed as he set the brake and came around the wagon to help her down.

She fought the smile that would show her amusement. "No, and I hope no one heard you." She took a deep breath and squared her shoulders. "Have I told you how grateful I am?"

Scott took her elbow in his hand and walked beside her to the church steps. "There's no need." He opened the door, leaving her no opportunity to continue the conversation.

Mildred Gillis's earnest efforts at the piano while the congregation sang a familiar hymn filled the air. Rena suspected the hymns played by her at the Gran Colina church were livelier than when they were played somewhere else. The preacher's wife was nothing if not energetic.

Several people turned to look as they entered, and Scott ushered her into a bench near the back of the church. He pulled out a hymnbook and held it for them to share. When she didn't sing, he raised his eyebrows in a questioning manner. The stares and disruption of the service by their entrance kept her from remembering the role she needed to play. She forced a smile at him and took the other side of the hymnbook. Her alto blended with his tenor voice for only a moment before the song ended.

Reverend Gillis invited everyone to take a seat. "Please bow your heads for prayer."

The words he prayed did not enter Rena's mind. She peeked around the room with her head bent forward. More than once she was greeted by a curious eye or sweet smile from a friend or acquaintance. It didn't seem honest to sit in the church, married to the sheriff and pregnant. She squeezed her eyes shut and asked the Lord to help her keep a pure and honest heart. She would not tarnish her newfound forgiveness by living a life of deception.

While the preacher delivered his message of love

and sharing, her mind raced through the last few weeks. She knew before they stood to sing the closing hymn that she had to speak to Scott alone. And she had to do it before they spoke to anyone else.

Rena tugged on his arm to get his attention. He leaned close, and she whispered, "I need to speak to you."

He nodded. "The service will be over soon."

"Now."

His brows drew together, but he closed the hymnbook and put it on the bench. He stepped into the aisle and waited for her to precede him out of the building. Outside he turned to her. "Is something wrong?"

"I can't live a lie."

Scott jerked his head to look in all directions. He spoke in low tones. "What are you talking about?"

Rena shook her head. "I can't do it. I can't expect God to forgive me for my sins, and then pretend to the entire town that you and I are happily married."

"Let's step away from the door of the church. People will be coming out soon."

They walked to the side of the building. Her words came tumbling out. "I'm sorry. I thought I could do it. I thought I could accept my forgiveness and move on, but I feel so guilty." Her heart was racing. "Any minute my father will be coming out of the church. He'll shake your hand and kiss me on the cheek. Then he'll ask how we're settling into married life."

Scott leaned close so he was almost eye level with her. "And you'll tell him that we're settling down just fine."

"But it's a lie." She wrung her hands and began to pace in front of him. "We aren't settling. We aren't happily married."

He caught her by the shoulders. "We are married, Rena. We are settling into married life."

"Not like everyone else does. We're pretending. We weren't even friends. Not true friends." She hated the thought of what she was saying. Tears blurred her vision, and she swallowed a sob.

"Rena. Stop it."

She caught her breath.

"Are married?"

"Yes."

"Are you settling in at the homestead? Getting your bearings and learning how to live there?"

She could only nod. Words would not come around the lump in her throat.

"What makes you think the people in that church are any different than us?"

"Those couples married for love. They wanted to have a life together."

He laughed. Laughed out loud.

"Don't you laugh at me, Scott Braden. I'm serious. We have to do something. I can't be a liar. Not on top of all I've already done. It wouldn't be honest before God."

"Do you honestly believe that Reverend Gillis married Mrs. Gillis because he fell in love and couldn't imagine his life without her?"

"I do."

"What about Ingrid Jefferson? Do you think her

new hats and fancy clothes mean that she's happily married to Jack Jefferson? Was that marriage a union of love and romance?"

"Oh, I don't know. She's so self-important."

"Jack is one of the most manipulative and controlling men I've ever known. Doubtless, his wife was someone who came from money and brought it with her when she married him. Are they living a lie?"

She shook her head. The tears dried up as she considered his words.

"We aren't lying, Rena. We live in a time where people marry for all kinds of reasons. I needed your help on the homestead. You needed me." She was relieved when he didn't expound on that thought. "We are married. We are settling into a new life together."

"You don't think it's dishonest?"

"I don't. We pledged our lives to one another in front of many of the people in that church. I meant the words I said to you then." He slid his hands from her shoulders to her elbows. "Did you speak your vows to me in honesty?"

She looked down at her hands. Her best gloves were twisted from the way she'd rubbed them together in stress. "I did."

"Then it's not a lie." He lifted one hand and, with his knuckle, tilted her chin until their eyes met. "We are friends. It's a new friendship, but I think we are going to be fine together. If you'll give us time."

She stared into his blue eyes and believed him. More than she'd believed anything Eugene had ever said to her. "Thank you, Scott. I'm sorry for putting you in this position."

"Shh. We already covered that."

The sound of the doors of the church opening echoed around the corner of the building. "Services must be over." She couldn't look away from him. The kindness he showed her was undeserved. It was more than any woman like her could expect.

"It seems so." He leaned close. "In friendship, will you allow me to kiss your cheek in front of the people who are watching from behind me?" A smile tugged on his crooked mouth.

She giggled. "Can you feel them staring, or is that a sort of sheriff's instinct, like when you knew I'd walked up behind you at the corral last night?"

"A little of both." He smiled and pressed his lips to her cheek. The contact was warm and gentle. It lasted long enough to show his care for her but was short enough to be respectful in a public setting.

Her father's voice bounded to them on the breeze. "Rena! Scott! There you are. Come give your pa a hug. And I want you and Scott to come straight by the house. We'll have a fine lunch."

When her father released her, and she greeted the townsfolk who stopped to speak, Rena was able to answer their questions in truth. Yes, she was happy. She was happy to be settled and have her father and Scott's reputations protected. She was happy to have a home and husband for her child's sake.

Dared she admit to herself that she was happy to have a friend in Scott? Someone who would protect her and provide for her. It was more than she'd thought possible in recent weeks.

She remembered the verse in the book of Psalms. *The lines are fallen unto me in pleasant places; yea, I have a goodly heritage.*

God had placed her safely in a place where, even if she didn't have romantic love, she was safe. She would be grateful.

Jack and Ingrid Jefferson cut across their path as Scott and Rena headed to their wagon on the far side of the churchyard.

"Where were you last night when the gunfight broke out?" Jack Jefferson's accusing stare narrowed in on Scott.

"Eli Gardner was on duty. He was around the corner from the saloon and heard the shots."

"Everybody in town knows that Eli Gardner is only the deputy because you and the mayor keep him around."

Scott's expression tightened, and he looked around the churchyard before turning back to Mr. Jefferson. "I'm sure the reverend and the ladies would rather we held this conversation at another time." He hooked his hand into the crook of Rena's arm. "If you'll excuse me, I'm going to take my wife to visit with her father."

Jefferson raised his voice as they walked away. "They'll all be wanting answers if the man who got shot dies. Up and marrying on the spur of the moment doesn't give you the right to neglect your duties. Seems to me like we need a new sheriff in this town."

Scott stopped and spun around to face Jefferson. He

opened his mouth, paused and closed it again. Without saying a word, he pivoted and walked away.

Rena heard the murmurs and whispers coming from the churchgoers who'd heard Jack Jefferson's angry words. Scott helped her into their wagon and headed the team toward her father's house. "Do you think the man will die?"

Scott shrugged his shoulders. "Doc said we won't know for a day or so."

"What do you think? You saw the man, didn't you?"

"I did, but only God knows how these things will go."

"He's right. You'll be blamed because you were with me." It was the last thing she wanted. Scott's name in the community shouldn't suffer because of her. If people knew what he was sacrificing for them, and for her, they wouldn't be so quick to judge him.

"It won't matter. As long as I do what the Good Book says, God will handle the rest." He glanced sideways at her. "Right now, the verse about being swift to hear and slow to speak is a bit hard to follow."

Rena looked over her shoulder and saw several people standing around Jack and Ingrid Jefferson. In her heart, she knew her husband was the topic of their conversation.

Scott had shown great restraint when he'd walked away without a word. She wasn't sure she'd ever be so close to God that she'd be able to do that.

"Papa was right about you."

He wrinkled his brow. "What?"

"You're a man of integrity. The people of Gran Colina are blessed to have a man like you for their sheriff." She was surprised to hear her next words. "I'm very proud of you."

Chapter Six

Scott didn't know how to respond to Rena's praise. Before he could think of something to say, he noticed a commotion in front of them at the center of town.

"Sheriff! Come quick!" Eli Gardner waved him forward.

He pulled the wagon to a stop at the corner. "What's the matter?"

Several people who had just left the church gathered in the middle of the street. Beyond the growing crowd, he saw Doc Taylor standing on the porch in front of his office. He climbed from the wagon and told Rena to wait for him.

"Doc said that fella just died." Eli pointed toward the townsfolk. "He was telling me when Jack Jefferson's buggy was passing in the street. He overheard and stopped to spread the word faster than a wildfire."

"Jefferson was already riling up people in the churchyard."

"I could tell the doctor didn't want everyone to

know before you found out. And the prisoner is still passed out drunk in his cell."

Scott clapped Eli on the shoulder. "Thanks, Eli. You go back to the jail, and I'll find out from the doc what happened."

Jefferson was waiting at the steps at the bottom of the doctor's office. "I told you no good would come of this. People being murdered in Gran Colina while you're not even in town is all the proof that I need you aren't fit to be sheriff."

"I'm going to have a word with Doc Taylor." Scott brushed aside Jefferson's attempts to distract him and motioned for the doctor to join him inside.

"Sorry, Sheriff." Doc Taylor closed the office door on the noise in the street. "He never came out of it. You never know when a fella is gut shot. He lost a lot of blood before we got to him. I did all I could."

"I know you did, Doc. I wish he could have told us his side of things." Scott looked out the front window and watched as word of the man's death spread among the people. "It's always a sad day when someone dies. It sadder still when that death becomes a tool to a man on a mission."

"Mr. Jefferson is a stubborn sort. Folks know you didn't have anything to do with this."

"That's exactly what he's out there telling everyone right now. That I did not have anything to do with preventing this man's death." He turned from the window. "Guess I better get a look at the body. I'll be contacting the judge, too."

After the doctor showed him the victim, they came

back into the front of the office. The door opened, and Rena entered in a huff. "Won't that man ever stop? A man has been killed, and all he can do is try to use the moment to discredit you."

Somehow, her disgruntled demeanor at the personal attack against him gave him comfort. It had been a long time since a woman had come to his defense. "The truth always comes out. Don't let them get to you."

The mayor came into the office then. "What a commotion. And on a Sunday of all days" Oscar disdained anything that went against his idea of an orderly town.

"Death doesn't know the day of the week." Doc Taylor spoke from experience. "I'm sure the man who passed this morning had no idea when he went into the saloon yesterday that he'd be gone today."

Rena peered out the front window. "Someone needs to go out there and stop Jack Jefferson or he'll have the whole town turned against both of you."

"I'll go." Her father moved toward the door.

Scott followed him. "I'll come with you."

Scott wasn't surprised when Rena followed them outside. The doctor stood in the open doorway.

"Now, folks, let's just simmer down." Oscar held both arms out and made a downward motion with his hands.

"A man's been murdered in our midst!" Cyrus Busby's reddened face drew Scott's attention. "Why should we calm down?"

Oscar wore his mayor persona like a comfortable coat. With calm tones, he tried again. "The good doctor has told us that, yes, this poor soul has passed away." A rumble of concern spread to the crowd. "But there's no need for everyone to get upset."

"Upset? The death of a man doesn't upset you?" Once again, Jack Jefferson took advantage of any opportunity to belittle the mayor.

"That's enough, Jefferson. We all know Oscar well enough to know that he does not discount the value of a man's life. I'm sure he was trying to say that we should not be upset because the man who did this evil deed is, at this moment, sitting in the town jail. There's no need for anyone to be stirring up fear or distress among us."

"Why should we listen to you? You weren't even in town when this happened."

Scott couldn't see who hurled the accusation, but he knew many of them were probably thinking the same thing. "There are some things in this life that cannot be prevented. Yes, I was at home last night with my new bride, but Eli Gardner was on duty." He cut his eyes to Rena. He hated to push her into the forefront of the matter, but she was already there. Letting people know he wanted to be home with her would work in their favor. Realizing the fact that he had truly wanted to be there with her was something he chose to ignore. There were more pressing issues at hand. He'd think about that later. If at all.

"What are you gonna do about Mabel's Saloon?" Alfred Murray's stutter became pronounced as he spoke. "It needs to be shut down."

Elmer Hicks stepped onto the first step of the doctor's porch. "You can't shut me down, Sheriff. I didn't shoot that man. Those two men were gonna fight no matter what anyone said. It's not my fault."

Scott would love to rid the town of the saloon, but he had no cause. "My job is to uphold the law. I can't close down the business without a legal reason."

"I just don't feel safe in Gran Colina anymore." Betty Alexander lived alone above the post office.

Oscar took a step forward. "Miss Alexander, I understand your concern, but this town is much safer than it was before Scott Braden became our sheriff."

"Of course you'll defend him. He's your new son-in-law." Jack Jefferson wore a smug look.

Scott wasn't surprised by Jefferson's attempts to malign Oscar or him. "Neither of these men is from Gran Colina. They got off the train yesterday afternoon. From all accounts, they were traveling together. I've got a notion that this dispute started long before they got to our town." Scott could tell that no good would come of a continued conversation. "Let's all go home now. The man responsible is in jail, and the judge will be here in the next few weeks. No one is in any danger."

Gilbert Jefferson laughed. "I'm guessin' that's what you were thinking when you went home on a Saturday night. Weren't any killings when I was sheriff."

"I'm not going to stand in the street and argue with you, Gilbert. I have work to do. I'll be in my office if anyone needs me."

"At least we'll know where to find you if someone

else dies." Gilbert goaded him, but Scott refused to acknowledge the spiteful remark.

The people dispersed a few at a time, and Scott turned to Rena. "Would you go to your father's and have lunch? I need to check in on the prisoner. I'll try to stop by in a little bit."

Rena put a gloved hand on his arm. "Are you sure you won't come eat first?"

"The last thing I need is for people to think I'm not doing my job today." He looked at Oscar. "I'm sorry, but at least the two of you can enjoy your meal."

Oscar nodded. "Come to the house when you finish." He took Rena's elbow in his hand. "Let's let the man do his job. We can keep a plate warm for him."

Scott headed for his office. The mood of the crowd today let him know that Oscar had been right. Any hint of impropriety by either of them would result in a loss come election day.

Rena paced in front of the fireplace in her father's parlor. "Papa, he stands to lose so much for having married me." She wrapped her arms around her middle and took a deep breath.

"Scott can handle this. He's faced a lot of difficult situations over the last couple of years." Oscar sat in his chair with an open book in his lap. He had abandoned any attempt to read due to her constant interruptions.

She stopped in front of the window and looked for any sign of Scott in the street outside. "But if anyone finds out why we got married, it will all be over."

They'd finished their lunch almost two hours earlier. Waiting was a part of life for a sheriff's wife. A part she didn't like.

"That's a risk he was willing to take."

"It's not fair to him." Why hadn't she considered these possibilities before she agreed to her father's plan?

"Life isn't fair, Rena. That's why God wants men like Scott in a position to do good. Scott helps to right the wrongs in our world."

"I just hope I haven't ruined everything for him." She turned to look at her father. She knew the strength to face him came from her growing faith. "I don't know how to tell you how sorry I am." She blinked away fresh tears.

Oscar stood and hugged her. "It's time to move on. You are forgiven. By God and by me. You'll need all your strength to get you through the coming months. Your marriage and baby are the most important things right now. We've done all we can about the election. The rest is in the hands of God." He dropped a kiss on the top of her head and released her.

"Thank you, Papa. Please pray for me, and I will pray for you and for Scott."

Her father was right. It was time to move on. She had to focus on Scott and her father. There would be time before the election to recover from the stress of this horrible murder.

Scott had rescued her and her child. She would do everything in her power to help him now.

* * *

Rena was putting their breakfast on the table the next morning when Scott entered the cabin. A cool breeze followed him inside.

"That smells delicious." He added the firewood he carried to the stack on the hearth. "Feels like it will be cold today."

"I'll be continuing to clean the cabin today, so I'll be warm."

He joined her at the table, and after offering thanks for their food, he filled his plate with fried ham, scrambled eggs and biscuits. "Before you get started on that I want to teach you to shoot."

"To shoot? Do I need to learn now? Can't it wait?"

"After what happened in town yesterday, I want to be sure you can protect yourself. You'll be here a lot when I'm not around." He buttered a biscuit and added blackberry jam that Ann had left in the cupboard. "Everyone on a homestead needs to know how to shoot."

Rena shook her head. "I don't know how good I'll be. I've never handled a gun before."

"I think you'll be a quick study. I taught Ann, too."

"Okay, but I hope it doesn't take a long time. I have a lot of cleaning to do."

Scott looked around the room. "You've already done so much. Make sure to take care of yourself and not work too hard."

"I'm not sick. I'm having a baby." Saying it aloud pulled at her heart. Talking about the baby in a normal conversation was strange and a bit terrifying. "I hope to be able to do my chores right up until the baby comes."

"All I'm saying is that there is no hurry. No need to wear yourself out."

She shouldn't have snapped at him. "I'm sorry. I don't mean to be so stubborn. You've been very kind, and I appreciate your concern. It's important to me to fulfill my promise to you. That's all I'm doing."

"No need to apologize. We're both doing that. Teaching you to shoot is another way for me to help protect you."

Rena tried to eat a good breakfast. Some mornings it was almost impossible. She suspected she would need her strength today.

An hour later, Scott lined up a row of old tins on a board he'd nailed between two fence posts. She studied him as he walked back in her direction. His determined gait mirrored his focus. Whenever he put his mind to something, he accomplished it.

"Now you're gonna hold the gun like I taught you and squeeze the trigger slowly. Remember, the gun is doing all the work. You only have to squeeze the trigger."

"Do I really need such a big gun?" The rifle he'd taught her to clean at the kitchen table was almost as long as she was tall.

"A rifle is more accurate at longer distances. If you're in the house, you can prop it in the window. It's easier to steady than a pistol. You'll need to learn to shoot holding the gun under your full strength, but most of the time you'll be able to use something for support."

He showed her again how to hold the gun. "It's loud, so don't let it startle you."

"I want you to shoot first. I want to hear it and see how you aim."

"Okay." Scott pulled the lever to load it and settled the butt of the rifle in front of his shoulder. He leaned his cheek over the top of the gun and pointed at the cans in the distance. She didn't think he moved until she heard the loud report and saw the rifle kick against his shoulder.

She squealed, jumped backward and clapped her hands over her ears. Scott lowered the gun into a safe position and laughed.

"I warned you about the noise."

Rena lowered her hands and squared her shoulders. "Well, now I'm ready. Show me what to do."

Scott handed her the gun, and she positioned it the same way he had. He pushed her elbow up to raise the level of the barrel. "There. Now look through the sight at the can on the left."

The gun was heavy, and the barrel lowered as her arms tired while she tried to focus on the can. Each time the barrel drifted downward, Scott pushed against her elbow.

"I think I'm ready."

"Then pull the lever to load the chamber."

She followed his instructions and waited until he stepped back, then squeezed the trigger. The recoil sent her stumbling backward. Scott caught her with one arm to keep her from falling. A cloud of dust half-way between her and the target showed how badly she missed.

"Not bad for your first shot." He took the gun and pointed it toward the ground.

It was her turn to laugh. "So shooting at the dirt will make the bad guys dance and run away?"

"Probably not, but it was good for your first try." He scratched the side of his jaw and thought for a minute. "Let's try something else. Here, you hold this." He gave the gun back to her and walked toward the barn.

She tried to draw a bead on the cans again while she waited on him. Her hair kept falling across her eyes and getting in her way. She blew it out of her face as he came back rolling a barrel. He kicked it up straight and rapped the top of it with his knuckles.

"You'll have to get down on one knee, but try steadying your arms on this."

When she was in position, she was able to hold the barrel still. "This is much better. I think I'm ready to try again." Scott backed away, and she fired.

The recoil of the weapon struck hard against her shoulder, but she didn't lose her balance this time. The cloud of dust from her shot was much closer to the fence line.

"Okay. I think I see what's going wrong." Scott knelt down beside her and, with both hands, pulled her shoulders straighter. "That's better." He pushed the barrel to the right and adjusted the butt of the rifle against her shoulder. "Now look at that second tin from the right."

"I see it."

He pushed the angle of the barrel up slightly. "Is that aimed at the top of the tin now?"

"Just above the top." She cut her eyes to the left, and his nearness surprised her. She'd been so focused on getting her aim right that she hadn't realized his arms encircled her. "Um, do I need to lower it?" She'd never been in the arms of a man, save the one night with Eugene. The shame of it flooded her mind, and heat filled her face.

Scott leaned away from her. Had he shared her thoughts? She knew her sin made her unacceptable to any man. That didn't stop the hurt she felt when her husband moved away.

He shook his head. "Uh, no, I think the rifle is shooting a little bit high. If you aim just above it, by the time your shot gets to the target it will have dropped. It should make for a direct hit."

Rena worked the lever to load the gun and rested her elbows on the barrel again. She looked back through the sight and found her mark. "Okay."

"Wait." Scott twisted her right shoulder back and her left shoulder forward. "Try that. It should protect your shoulder." He stood and backed away from her.

She could breathe again. Having him near—being near any man—was unsettling. Knowing that he didn't want to be there was understandable, and disheartening.

With a few more shots, she was able to gain enough accuracy to satisfy Scott. He also spent a few minutes teaching her how to shoot a revolver.

"You know enough now to be safe." He put the revolver in the holster he wore on his hip. "I'll put the rifle back over the fireplace. There are extra bullets in a box on the mantel."

She followed him as he walked toward the house. "I hope I never need it."

"Me, too." He checked the position of the sun in the sky before he stepped onto the porch. "I'm going to head into town. The outside chores are done. I may be late, so don't hold supper for me."

Rena stood at the kitchen window, washing their breakfast dishes, and watched him ride up the lane. They'd only been married a few days, and he was already planning to be out late. It wasn't fair to expect him to come home eagerly in the evenings. Their marriage wasn't like that. In any case, as sheriff, his work would often demand late hours.

She made a mental list of all the things she would do today and hoped it would keep her mind off the lonely days she knew were in her future.

When Scott came home after nine that night, a faint light flickered in the front window of the cabin. He hoped Rena had left a lamp on for him and gone to bed.

He put his horse in the stall and noticed that all the animals had been fed and watered. He hadn't meant to add extra work for her. The next time he had to work late, he'd send one of the Henderson boys over to take care of the chores.

Scott sat on the porch steps and took off his boots. He moved with extra care and opened the door. Rena was asleep in the rocker in front of the fire. The lamp that burned was on a small table at her elbow. He closed the door as softly as he could, but she stirred from her rest.

"Oh, it's you." She rubbed the sleep from her eyes with one hand and closed the Bible in her lap with the other. "Let me get your supper."

He motioned for her to stay where she was. "I'll get it." He didn't have the heart to tell her he'd eaten hours earlier. Truth be told, he'd worked so long that he welcomed the late meal.

"Let me make some coffee. I'm afraid I finished the pot after supper. I was going to make more, but I didn't think I'd fall asleep." She was beside him at the stove. "I hope there wasn't any trouble in town today." She added water to the coffeepot and set it on the stove to heat.

"No new trouble." He took the plate she'd covered with a towel and sat at the table. "I sent the judge a telegram to tell him about the killing. I hope to hear back from him by the end of the week. It'll sit better with folks if they know when he'll be in town."

She turned from the stove. "Do you think he'll change his schedule for such an important case? Surely a murder would warrant his immediate attention."

He cut a bite of ham from the generous portion she'd prepared. "It depends on his other cases. I hope so. I'd like this settled and done long before the election."

"Did you see Papa today?"

"Yes. He came by to see about the prisoner. We

don't usually have anyone in the cells for more than a day or so."

"How was he?"

"He's fine. He's more anxious than I am to see this business behind us."

She busied herself getting cups and sugar for their coffee. She was graceful to watch. Peaceful after a day in the midst of accusations and listening to the fears of the townsfolk he'd encountered.

"I'm glad you weren't in town today. Several people came by the office with one excuse or another. Their true motive was to get a glimpse at the prisoner."

"I'm sorry." She put coffee cups on the table and unwrapped a basket filled with tea cakes. She offered it to him and took one for herself.

"It's to be expected. I think most of them want to make sure the man isn't someone they know. They want to put their minds at ease. Can't say as I blame them." He took a drink of the coffee and held it up to her. "Umm…this is good."

"Thank you." She broke off a piece of her tea cake and nibbled at it.

"There is one odd thing. About the prisoner."

Rena sat straighter in her chair. "What is it?"

He debated whether he should tell her or not, but he hoped another perspective could help them sort through the details. "He told every person the same story he told me on Saturday night. He insists that the man he killed was the aggressor."

"Isn't that common? Especially when one person isn't able to tell their side of the story."

"At first that's what I thought, but he keeps saying it the same way. He says the man started the argument with him at a card table. He told me the other man had a gun pointed at him under the table, but there was no gun in the saloon when Eli got there. He's a good deputy. I know he did a thorough search. I didn't find one either."

"So he must be lying?"

"See, there's another question about it, too. It's eating at me. If he'd fumbled the story or told it in different ways, I could dismiss it."

"What are you going to do?"

"I don't know if it'll do any good, but I'm going to talk to other people who were there that night. If someone else saw a gun, then I need to know what happened to it."

She was thoughtful. He liked that she didn't jump to a conclusion like so many people would. "I pray you find the truth. It would be awful for the man to be convicted of a murder if he was defending himself."

"It would also be wrong for him to tell a tale to escape punishment."

"I don't envy you. I had not considered how difficult this part of your job could be. You need the wisdom of Solomon to handle situations like this."

It was difficult. He wouldn't deny it. "Yes. There are some times when only God knows the truth."

Her brow wrinkled. "I know these two men were strangers to Gran Colina, but every man deserves to be judged by the facts of a matter. Do you think the townspeople will be more upset if you look into this man's claims?"

He nodded. "Some of them well may be, but it's my duty to find the truth. Even if it's inconvenient or troublesome. If no one else saw a gun or witnessed the dead man provoking the prisoner, he'll have a hard time in front of the judge. And with the fury that Jack Jefferson is trying to stir up in town, even if I find the gun or witnesses, the jury may already think he's guilty."

"That would be terrible."

"I'll see what I can find out tomorrow." He was surprised at the relief he felt by sharing the information with her. The more he thought about it, the more he realized there could be something about the events of Saturday night that hadn't come to light yet.

Scott didn't want the last thing they talked about that night to keep Rena awake. She needed her rest. He would do his duty, but, for now, he would change the subject. "How was your day? Are you feeling better?"

"I finished the inside of the house. I'll start on the outside of the windows tomorrow."

He sputtered his coffee and set his cup down. "You'll what?"

"I need to clean the windows from the outside."

"No, you don't. I'll do that."

"Our agreement was for me to take care of the cabin and you to take care of the homestead and be the sheriff."

"My agreement was to take care of you—" his eyes involuntarily moved to her midsection "—and the child." He turned his gaze to the fireplace to avoid her stare. "I have no intention of letting you climb a ladder and wash windows."

"Letting me?" She twisted her coffee cup on the table. "You won't let me?" The way her voice rose let him know he'd upset her. The same way he used to upset Ann. He should have learned how to word things by now.

"I mean, I don't want you to get hurt. I think it's best if you let me take care of the ladder and the windows."

"I won't get hurt. I'm not as round as a house yet. I can still balance on a ladder. It's only a little bit out of my reach. One or two rungs of the ladder at most."

"Will you at least let me put the ladder against the house for you?" This woman was a stubborn one. If only she'd resisted Eugene Rodgers the way she resisted him.

The thought was unfair, and he regretted it as soon as it went through his mind. Eugene had tricked her. Scott was sure of that. His smooth-talking ways had irked Scott the first time he'd met the man.

"You can put the ladder out for me, but I will wash the windows." She seemed to be satisfied with that.

"Okay. I'll put it out in the morning. First thing." He would be in the barn watching through the door while she worked, but he was too smart to tell her that.

He finished his supper and pushed his chair back. The tea cakes were delicious, and he wanted to savor them while he drank his coffee. "I'm sorry I was so late. You didn't need to wait up. You must be exhausted."

"I was reading." She gathered his dishes and put them in the basin.

"I'm sorry you had to do the chores, too." He bit into another tea cake.

"It didn't take long. I hope I did everything right."

"Nothing seemed amiss when I put Copper in his stall." He picked up the last tea cake and his coffee cup. "Will you sit with me for a few minutes?" He sat on the hearth in hopes that the warmth would seep through to his bones and take away the chill that the ride home had caused.

Rena sat in her rocking chair and set it in motion with the toe of her shoe. When had Ann's chair become hers in his mind? Each day a part of his life was adjusting to her. That was probably a good thing, but the ease with which he was unconsciously accepting her presence surprised him.

"You were reading the Bible?"

She nodded and ran her hand across the worn cover of her Bible on the table. "It was my mother's. Papa gave it to me."

"What a precious gift." He watched her pick it up and open it.

"She made notes on the pages." She flipped through several of them. "When I read it, I can almost hear her teaching me the lessons of the verses. I should have paid more attention when she read to me and Papa every night." She turned another page. "If I had, I wouldn't have deserted her faith when she died. I'd have realized that her faith could be mine. That I'll see her again when it's my time to leave this world."

She sniffed. "Then I wouldn't have stopped going to church and allowed myself to—"

"Don't, Rena." He wanted to take her in his arms and comfort her, but he didn't think she'd appreciate his efforts. Not after the way she'd reacted during the shooting lesson earlier in the day. "You can't judge yourself on what could have been. God meets you where you are."

She followed the words on the page with a fingertip. "I know that now."

Scott didn't know how to respond to her. What she'd said was true. The teachings of her mother's faith would have spared her the pain inflicted by Eugene Rodgers. But she hadn't believed in God's ways when she'd met the scoundrel. He couldn't ease her pain, but maybe he could distract her. "It's been a long day. Why don't you try to get some rest? I was thinking you might like to ride into town with me tomorrow. I know you're not accustomed to being so isolated. Maybe you could meet Charlotte for lunch or visit with your father."

The words had the desired effect. "I'd like that. I'll need to wash the windows first." She smiled and stood.

"I worked late today. As long as I'm in the office before lunch tomorrow, that will be fine."

"Can I get you anything else?"

"No. I'm going to bed in a few minutes myself."

He returned her smile, and watched as she walked into her room. The soft click of the door closing echoed the separation he felt whenever he was with her. They were in the same house, sharing a homestead, but their lives couldn't be more apart.

She had come to faith when she found herself in a desperate situation. It was natural for people to turn to God in tragic circumstances. He prayed her faith would grow and flourish. More trouble often caused those same people to abandon God just as quickly as they'd embraced Him.

Chapter Seven

Rena pretended that she didn't notice Scott watching from the barn as she washed the windows. She wanted to laugh at his overprotectiveness, but something deep inside of her warmed at the thought that someone cared about her. It was nice. She knew he didn't care for her in the way of most husbands, but it was more than she had expected for herself after she realized she was pregnant.

She dragged the ladder to the last window and climbed up two rungs. She was tired, but this would end the extra work she'd had to do since she'd come to the homestead. They might be living on an untamed land, but she wanted their home to be in order.

The top corner of the last pane was almost out of reach, but she stretched and finished the job. On the ground again, she backed up to admire her handiwork.

"They look great." Scott's voice was so near that it caused her to jump.

"Thanks. I didn't realize you were behind me." She

wrung out her cleaning rag and tossed the dirty water from her bucket into the side yard. "Though I did see you watching from the barn." She smiled and headed for the porch when he rolled his eyes.

He was carrying the ladder to the barn. "I was making sure you didn't miss anything." His laughter followed her up the cabin steps.

"I'll be ready to go to town in a few minutes."

When they arrived in Gran Colina, he stopped in front of the hotel so she could have lunch with Charlotte. He helped her from the wagon.

"Enjoy your visit. I'll be at the office when you finish."

"After lunch I'm going to see my father, and there are a couple of things that I need from the mercantile."

"Put whatever you need on our account."

It didn't feel right for him to pay for everything she needed. She took a step closer to him and spoke in a low voice. "I'm stopping by to see Papa about what I need."

His blue eyes narrowed. He caught his bottom lip between his teeth and took a breath. "You are my wife, Rena. I will pay for whatever you need. I would appreciate it if we do not have this discussion again in the future."

His tone brooked no argument. "Okay. I meant no disrespect. I only need a few things for cooking and some fabric to make curtains for my room."

"Get what you need." He angled his head to one side. "Do you sew? I thought you only mended." He seemed doubtful.

She shook her head. "It's not a skill that I've mastered. I'm able to do basic things, but nothing as elaborate as, say, a dress."

The front door of the hotel opened, and Charlotte came onto the sidewalk. "There you are. I was wondering when you would come to town again."

"I've come to have lunch with you." Rena stepped onto the sidewalk. "If you think your mother can spare you."

"Yes. Tuesdays are not quite so busy. I'll go let her know you're here." Charlotte left them.

Rena turned back to Scott. "I'll be frugal."

"I am not without funds, Rena. As long as you're not prone to extravagance, it will be fine."

As he climbed into the wagon and rode away, Rena wished the little things weren't so challenging. Any newly married couple would face the same kinds of daily decisions that she and Scott faced. The only difference was that she knew she had no right to ask him for anything else. He'd already done more for her than any man in her life, save her father.

Lunch with Charlotte was refreshing after the days of hard work on the homestead. Charlotte caught her up on little tidbits of town gossip and quizzed her, without success, about her life with Scott.

"I just can't believe you won't even give me a morsel of news. I'm your dearest friend. How will I know what to expect of married life if you never share with me?" Charlotte's lighthearted approach to any situation made Rena a little bit sad. Rena envied her innocence and dreams of fairy-tale stories. Her parents, especially her mother, protected her from many of the harsh truths of life.

Not wanting to disappoint her, Rena said, "Well, I can tell you that cleaning a cabin after a man has lived in it alone for a couple of months will wear out a city girl."

"Oh no. Was it awful?" Charlotte leaned her elbows on the table and listened to every nuance of Rena's accounting of the cabin.

"But the worst part was the stove. I'm not sure he ever took a rag to it." She grimaced when she thought about the afternoon that she'd spent cleaning it. "I guess he thought the heat of the next cooking would burn off anything that had boiled over from another meal." They both laughed.

Charlotte's voice went soft. "Surely the other parts of married life—the kindness, the never being alone—make up for the hard work."

If only that were true. Scott was kind, but Rena was alone, in ways Charlotte would never understand. She searched her mind for a way to tell the truth without revealing matters that she and Scott had agreed to keep private.

"The security of having my life settled is comforting. The hard work will pay off in time." She lifted another bite of apple pie onto her fork. "At least I know the cabin will never be that dirty again."

It was pleasant to laugh and talk with Charlotte, but she needed to seek out her father if she was going to see him before Scott was ready to leave town.

Rena found him in front of the doctor's office.

"Hello, Papa." She stretched up on the toes of her shoes and put a kiss on his cheek. "How are you?"

"I'm fine." He smiled down at her. "I'm surprised to see you today. Scott didn't tell me you'd be coming to town."

"I needed some things from the mercantile, and I wanted to see Charlotte." She looked over his shoulder and, through the window, saw the doctor at his desk. "You're not ill?"

"No. I dropped by to see if Doc Taylor wanted to come by the house after supper and play a game of chess." He looked away from her. "The evenings can be long and quiet."

"Oh, Papa. You miss me." She looped her arm through his, and they started walking toward Scott's office. "You can ride out and visit with Scott and me anytime you'd like."

"It wouldn't be right for me to intrude on your privacy so soon." He patted her hand on his arm. "What would people think?" His answer was serious. Her father would do everything in his power to keep up appearances and protect Gran Colina.

Being supportive of him was important to her. "Then don't beat the doctor too badly. You'll want him to come again soon."

Scott rose from the chair behind his desk when they entered the sheriff's office. "Good afternoon, Oscar."

Rena looked toward the cell on the back wall. A man was prone on the bed with his face toward the wall. A shudder ran up her spine. She'd never been in the same room with someone who'd taken a life.

"Have you been to the mercantile?" Scott moved to block her view of the prisoner when the man rolled over and sat up.

"Not yet." She leaned to see around him, but he put a hand on her arm and turned her toward her father.

"Oscar, would you mind escorting her to the mercantile. There is some shopping she needs to do."

Her father nodded. "If you think it's necessary."

"I do." Scott leaned close to her. "I don't want you to come back to the office until this man is gone. I should have arranged to meet you at your father's house." He ushered her outside. "I'll pick you up there after I leave here."

Rena stopped on the sidewalk. "I don't need you to protect me from everything, Scott. You said that many of the people in town have come to see him. Why should I be any different?"

"You may not like the idea of being protected, but I don't like the thought of a killer in the same room with my wife."

His wife. Did something change in a man when he took on the responsibility of a wife? She had married Scott, and she felt beholden to fulfill her commitment to care for his home and protect his reputation. Scott seemed to have taken on a deeper level of obligation.

"Okay." She peered through the window. "It is unsettling to think about."

"Then we're agreed." He released her elbow. "I'll see you in a couple of hours."

Rena spent the rest of the afternoon shopping for just the right items to make the cabin feel more like home. A new copper kettle to make tea for the cold winter nights when she didn't want coffee and a larger coffeepot were among her first selections. She also chose a large pan for baking cakes and bread.

The dark green fabric was her favorite purchase. The curtains she envisioned would cover the window and block out the sunlight when the baby napped. The lush richness of the green tone mirrored the tall pines that ran along the road in front of the homestead.

Satisfied that she hadn't spent too much money, she placed the last of the items on the counter and asked Cyrus to add them to her account.

Cyrus jotted the prices on a notepad and added them up with a pencil. "I still don't know how no one realized you and the sheriff were courtin'." He held up the fabric and called out to his wife across the shop. "How much for this?"

Ethel put a bolt of fabric back on the display table and walked to the counter. "I'll add this up." She took the pad and pencil from him and added the price of the fabric. "You know you shouldn't yell out across the store. People will think you're uncivilized." She tapped him on the nose with the pencil and smiled.

"Don't tell me how to act in my own business, woman." Cyrus backed away to give his wife room to work.

"It's our business, Cyrus." Ethel looked up at Rena. "And that's the only business we should be minding."

Rena smiled her gratitude for Ethel's consideration of her privacy.

Cyrus shook his head. "It don't make no sense.

One day you've got a sheriff who is all about his job and stays in town more than on his own spread. The next, you got a dead man at the doc's office and a killer in the jail." He made a clicking sound in his cheek. "Nope. Something's not right here. I feel it in my bones."

Rena would have taken her trade elsewhere if she could, but it would only feed Cyrus Busby's curiosity about her and Scott. "Mr. Busby, as a lady, I am loath to repeat the explanation my husband gave you last week to this very question."

Ethel swatted his shoulder. "You've gone and embarrassed her good now, Cyrus. You need to stop your jabbering about things that don't concern you." Ethel finished her sums and showed the amount to Rena.

"That's fine, thank you." Rena wanted to leave, but Ethel still had to wrap her purchases. She didn't want to risk ruining the fabric, or she'd pick it up and walk out this instant.

"A man gets notions, all right, but not someone like Scott Braden. He's kept a cool head through too much over the last two years. I might be willing to accept his story from the likes of somebody like Alfred Murray. Why, that barber would swallow his tongue if a woman looked at him sideways. But not the sheriff." Cyrus leaned against the cabinet behind the counter like a man with nowhere else to be. "What did you do to him, Mrs. Braden? Catch him stealing pie from the hotel restaurant? See him sneaking out of the saloon late one night? There had to be some motivation for a man as free as Scott Braden to up and marry on a whim."

The man had gone too far. "Mr. Busby, I will thank you to keep your opinions to yourself. Never, and I mean never, has my husband stolen so much as a crumb of pie. He does not make a habit of going to places where a good man wouldn't go, nor did I trap him into marriage as you suggest." Rena's voice rose with every word. Ethel Busby's face blanched pale, but Rena was beyond the point of stopping the tirade that gushed from her now. "Scott Braden's integrity is above reproach. I dare say you could learn a thing or two by patterning your behavior after his."

Rena gasped. She had not taken in air since the first word of her rebuke of the man. "Mrs. Busby, would you be so kind as to wrap my purchases and see they are delivered to my father's house? I'll be there for the next hour or so."

"I will, Mrs. Braden, and please forgive my Cyrus. Everyone knows he's a curious sort who doesn't always remember when to mind his tongue."

Rena looked at the man with his jaw hung wide, speechless after her reproof. "It's past time he learned to do just that."

She spun on her heel and almost lost her balance when she saw Scott standing in the open doorway of the store. His blue eyes were like steel. "Scott! I didn't know you were there."

"Rena. Mrs. Busby." Scott tipped his hat at the two ladies, then he turned to Mr. Busby. "Cyrus."

"Sheriff." If there wasn't a cabinet behind the man,

Rena had the distinct impression he'd have taken a step back.

"In other circumstances, I might feel compelled to come in here and defend my wife, but I see she's done that for the both of us." He held the door open and motioned for Rena to leave with him. "I trust that our business is important enough to you that we won't have to wonder whether this kind of event will occur in the future."

"No, sir, Sheriff Braden." Ethel stepped around the counter, wringing her work apron in her hands. "Please accept our apologies."

"You're kind, Mrs. Busby, but those apologies are due to my wife, and they will need to come from Cyrus."

"I'm sorry, Sheriff. Don't know what's got into me these last few days. I've just been thinking up all kinds of crazy things. Maybe it comes from being shut up inside the business day and night during these cold months."

"As I said, my wife is the one who deserves the apology." Scott stood still with his hand on the door.

Cyrus looked at his wife and back at Scott. He cleared his throat. "Mrs. Braden, please accept my apology. I spoke out of turn."

The muscle on Scott's jaw rippled, and Rena thought she heard him grind his teeth. She needed to bring calm to the situation. She'd meant to handle it without Scott ever having to know it happened.

"I accept, Mr. Busby. I will put it out of my mind and trust that you will, also."

"You're most gracious, Mrs. Braden." Ethel spoke the words, but at Scott's stare, Mr. Busby added his appreciation. "Thank you, ma'am."

In the street, Rena turned to Scott. "I'm so sorry you heard that."

He laughed. "I must say that you handled yourself very well." He held out his arm for her, and she looped her hand inside the crook of his elbow. "I'd hate to be on the receiving end of your wrath."

She smiled up at him. "I don't see that we'll have much to disagree about. We both have the same purposes. Protect each other, protect my father and protect Gran Colina."

Scott sobered. "You've proved to me today how determined you are to do just that."

As he walked her to her father's house, Rena realized how readily she had jumped to his defense. It wasn't a chore or pretense. Her automatic and genuine response surprised her. The week before it would've been calculated. Now it was instinctive.

The following Sunday afternoon Scott asked Rena to take a walk with him. "Let's get some fresh air. The weather is mild, and who knows how long it will be before we have another pretty day like this."

"Okay, let me just get a shawl. It will be nice to get outside for a change. In town, I was out and about almost every day. I find I spend most of my days inside while you're at work."

They walked toward the creek that ran through the valley behind the cabin.

Scott matched his pace to hers. "You might enjoy a walk in this direction during the afternoons."

"I may do that. Now that I've caught up on the chores, I should have some free time."

"You've done a great job. I'm sorry it was such a mess."

Rena laughed. "Thank you. It was a challenge, but I am sure there are much worse situations."

"I don't want to see them." He laughed with her.

Rena slowed her steps. "Have you discovered anything about the gun that you were looking for?"

"No. Nothing that makes sense. Elmer Hicks tried to remember everyone who was there that night. He said most of them are regulars who've come in since he opened the saloon. I've spoken with almost all of them."

"What are you going to do?"

"Pray, a lot. God knows the truth. I'm praying He will reveal it."

"I'll pray with you." Her words pleased him. When he had agreed to marry her, it never occurred to him that Rena would become someone he could share his problems with. Her prayers were an added benefit.

Her consideration came on the heels of finding her life turned upside down. He could only imagine how all the changes were affecting her. "What about you? I know you're not accustomed to being on your own so much."

"It's given me a lot of time to think."

That would explain her quietness over the last many days. "You don't seem to be yourself. Oh, you're fine when others are around—you even laugh. But it's not like before. Not like the times at your pa's house."

"I've had to grow up fast over the last couple of months. My carefree days are gone."

It was true. She was more sober and calm. He missed her good nature. He didn't miss the flightiness that he believed had made her vulnerable, but the gloom that hovered over her most days grieved him. "You don't have to be sad, Rena."

"I'm not sad." She pulled on the fringe of her shawl. "I was a child for too long. It was past time for me to grow up."

They had come to stand at the water's edge, and he turned to her. "You can be an adult, but you can be happy, too."

Rena gazed across the creek to the other side. "I don't deserve to be happy. After the confrontation with Mr. Busby in town last week, I realize that I'll never be able to escape what I've done. I'll always wonder who suspects, who saw something, who knows my secret."

"You can't live like that. Everyone has things in their past that they want to forget. You have to let it go."

Hopelessness weighed on her countenance. "I've tried. Even in church today, I prayed again, but the questions behind the stares are always there. Probing. I'm so afraid that God's forgiveness won't protect me from my guilt."

"That's not how God works. He forgives and forgets."

"But people don't. With people like Mr. Busby asking questions and stirring doubt, everything we've done can be ruined. I know God forgives. But if I can't forgive myself, how can I expect other people to forgive me?"

"Other people don't know." Scott stepped in front of her and put his hands on her shoulders. "And if the whole world finds out, and they never forgive you, it will only matter if you let it. God's forgiveness is all you'll ever need. You've got to believe that."

The smile she gave him was forced. "I'm trying."

"I have an idea." He slid his hands down to capture hers. "Sit with me." He took off his jacket, laid it out on the creek bank for her to sit on and sat beside her.

"What's your idea?"

He leaned back on his elbows. "I want you to tell me the most embarrassing thing that ever happened to you as a child."

"No! Why would I do that?"

"Trust me." He closed his eyes. "I won't even look at you while you tell me."

"What difference will that make? You'll still hear me."

"I'm not leaving until you tell me."

She made a scoffing sound. "Well, you may just have to stay here then."

He opened his eyes. "Do you trust me?"

Rena nodded.

"Then do this for me." He closed his eyes again. "Think about it. Was it saying something silly in front of the whole class? Did you fall in a mud puddle during recess and ruin a dress you'd worn to impress a boy in school? Oh! I know. You wrote a boy a note, and the teacher caught you. You had to read it out loud, and everyone laughed at you."

"No." She chuckled. "Nothing like that ever happened to me."

"Was it something worse?" He opened his eyes and sat up. "I'll go first." He held up one hand. "But you can't laugh. No matter what."

A smile tugged at the corners of her mouth. "No guarantees. Not if it's anything as silly as what you thought I might have done."

"You have to close your eyes."

She narrowed her eyes at him. "Okay, but only so I can't see you, not so you can trick me."

"No tricks." He stared at her until her eyes closed. "I was seven. My pa bought a donkey. He said it was stronger and cheaper than our old horse. The neighbors came to visit one Sunday afternoon. They had a boy named Mark. He was my friend, and I wanted to show him our new donkey. Pa warned me not to go in his stall. Mark teased me and said I was afraid of that donkey or I'd go in his stall. He called me a chicken."

"Oh no." She twisted her mouth to keep from laughing. "I think I can guess what you did."

"Well, you might guess part of it. Yes, I did go into the stall. That donkey wasn't used to anyone but Pa. He spun in a circle and tried to bite my hat. Round and round we went. Mark laughed and hollered. Our pas came into the barn and caught me in that stall. I knew I was going to be in trouble with Pa, but I had to get away from the donkey first. Every time I went

left, the donkey cut me off. I tried to go right, and he'd
spin again. I finally took off my hat and tried to shoo
him away by flapping it in his face."

"What was your pa doing?"

"Hanging over the stall door laughing. He said I
deserved whatever I got for going in there in the first
place." He watched her relax as she listened to his tale.
He'd tell it over and over again if it would make the
worry leave her face. "Well, that donkey didn't like
me slapping at him, so he snatched my hat with his
teeth and tossed it over his shoulder. I lunged to save
it. It was my Sunday hat."

"Uh-oh. Are we about to get to the most embarrassing part of this story?"

"Yes. I saved my hat, but I slid across that stall
floor on my belly like a fish on a slippery bank." She
started to giggle. "My pa laughed and laughed. Ma
even laughed, but then she made me wash those clothes
myself. It took three washings to get the smell of the
barn floor out of those pants. Ma finally gave up on
the shirt and had Pa bury it in the backyard."

Rena opened her eyes and laughed in earnest. "You
poor thing. Did your friend get in trouble?"

"Nope. Pa said I shouldn't let what someone else
says control my actions. He said if I'd been more concerned about minding my pa I wouldn't've been covered in barn dirt." He laughed with her. "I didn't think
I'd ever get clean again."

"What about the donkey? Did he ever get used to
you?"

"I never went in the stall with that donkey again.

If I had to clean it, I'd put him in the corral while I did the work."

Her smile reached her eyes. "Lesson learned." She sobered. "If only all of life's lessons would come out in the wash."

"Sometimes it takes more than one washing, and sometimes you have to bury your old stuff and move on." He watched as the truth of his words sank in. "You don't have to let the things that mortified you in the past follow you into your future. You can let them go. No matter how bad they are. Even if you get the stink of a thing all over you. Take a bath and keep living. Bad things happen to everyone. After it happens, all we can choose is how we'll let it affect us."

She looked over at him and smiled. "Thank you, Scott. I will endeavor to make wise choices."

Something like relief tugged on his soul. It gave him hope to see her put forth the effort needed to heal.

"That's good news." He sat up and rested his elbows on his knees. "Now. It's your turn. What was that embarrassing thing?"

"Oh, no you don't. Sharing your story made the point. I'm going to keep my embarrassment buried in the past, just like you said."

Her lightheartedness was genuine, so he gladly changed the subject. "Your appetite seems to be improving. You must be feeling better physically."

Rena nodded. "I am. It's been tough, but I hope I'm through the worst of it."

"That's good to hear." He stood and reached to help

her. "What do you say we go home and have another piece of that pie you made?"

"I like that idea." She put her hands in his, and he pulled her to her feet.

They stood for a moment, face-to-face, hand in hand. A subtle understanding passed between them. An unspoken acknowledgment of a new friendship bound them together in harmony. Today they had learned that they could support one another. Friendship had never been their goal, but it was nice to have.

Chapter Eight

By the end of February, Rena realized she would need some new clothes. She stood in front of the mirror in her room and tugged at the hem of her jacket. "There's no putting it off now."

"Putting off what?" Scott stood at the open door of her room.

"I didn't hear you come back in from the chores." She captured his gaze over her shoulder in the reflection of the mirror. He leaned against the doorjamb. "It's time to do something about my clothes." She rested her palms across the bottom of her jacket. "The things I have won't fit for much longer."

"Would you like to go to town with me this morning? You could purchase fabric and take it to the dressmaker. Or would you prefer to buy ready-made clothes?"

"I've been thinking about it. If I go to the dressmaker, perhaps I can choose patterns that can be altered after the baby comes. Then the money wouldn't be wasted."

"Whatever you think is best." He pointed over his shoulder. "I'll hitch up the wagon."

Wrapped in her heaviest cape, Rena rode beside Scott on the wagon seat. She shivered and lifted her collar up to warm her neck. "After the mild weather of the last few days, I wasn't prepared for this cold."

Scott held the reins in one hand and pointed with the other. "From the looks of those clouds, we may even get some snow."

"Brrr. I hope not." She rubbed her gloved hands up and down her arms in an effort to produce heat. "I much prefer Texas summers to bitter cold."

"I don't imagine it will last long. It rarely does."

"Did the judge ever send you a date for the trial?"

"I sent him another telegram yesterday. I hope to know this week."

Time was passing quickly. Almost six weeks had passed since they'd married, and the election was set for six weeks from today. "It needs to be soon or it could affect the election."

"It appears to be a simple case, even though the man still protests his innocence."

"I just wish you could've found someone who could vouch for the presence of another gun."

"I tried. It's all in God's hands."

Scott helped Rena from the wagon in front of the mercantile. "I'll be at my office if you need me."

She stood on the sidewalk and watched him ride away. Over the course of the last month, their friendship had grown. When they'd married, she would never have dreamed that she would be comfortable in an arranged marriage. The days on the homestead could be boring, but she was grateful for the security of their friendship.

Ethel Busby opened the door of the mercantile. "Won't you come in, Mrs. Braden?"

Rena watched as Scott climbed out of the wagon and went up the steps to the sheriff's office before responding. "Yes, thank you." She smiled at Ethel. "You know you don't have to call me Mrs. Braden."

Ethel's eyebrows went up, and she waved a finger at Rena. "You're a married lady. You deserve to have the title."

Rena held up a small piece of paper. "I need a few things for my cupboard to look at your fabric."

Ethel took the list from her. "Cyrus—" she waved for him to come from behind the counter "—will you gather the things Mrs. Braden needs while I help her find some fabric?"

Cyrus joined them near the front of the store. In the weeks since their confrontation, he maintained an air of polite indifference. "I'll get right on that." He nodded a greeting to Rena and walked briskly to the opposite side of the store.

Ethel coughed to cover a chuckle. "I've been meaning to thank you."

Rena pulled off her glove and rubbed her hand across a length of blue material. "For what?"

"Cyrus hasn't been the same man since the day you set him straight. It must've been two weeks before Betty Alexander could even tempt him with a morsel of gossip."

It was difficult not to laugh, but Rena tried. "I am sorry it came to that, but I won't apologize for protecting me or my husband."

"I think it was high time someone let Cyrus know how painful it is to others when you stick your nose where it doesn't belong." Ethel lifted a bolt of fabric from the opposite side of the table and unwound a length for Rena to inspect. "Let's see if we can't find you something pretty and forget about that stinker."

Rena chose several lengths of fabric, and Ethel wrapped them up for her. As she tied the string on the last package, Cyrus came from the storage room. "Would you like me to carry your order by the sheriff's office?"

"Thank you, Mr. Busby. That would be nice." Rena picked up the last parcel of cloth and bade them both goodbye.

She made her way down the street to the dressmaker's shop. A brass bell clanged as she entered and closed the door. "Hello? Are you busy, Mrs. Pennington?"

Opal Pennington pulled a curtain from the doorway near the rear of the shop and entered the room. "Hello, Mrs. Braden. What can I do for you today?"

Rena placed her parcels on the round oak table in the center of the room. "I find myself in need of some new clothes. I was hoping you could help me choose some new patterns."

"I'd be glad to."

Rena pulled off her cape and draped it across the back of a chair. She added her gloves and reticule to the pile of parcels on the table. "I hope you don't mind, but I've brought several lengths of fabric. If you're very busy, perhaps I can get one outfit at a time."

Opal tilted her head one way and then another as she studied Rena. She pulled one end of the measuring tape she wore around her neck. "If you'll just step back here, I can take your measurements, and we can get started." The dressmaker was known for her adept ability to size up a customer without her measuring tape. Rena knew that Opal would likely be the first person to recognize the changes in her body.

She followed Opal through the doorway and into the back room. Opal pulled the curtain across the opening and motioned for Rena to step up onto the platform in front of the large mirrors in the room. "I trust married life is treating you well." Opal pulled her first measurement at Rena's neck. With the pencil that she wore over her ear, she noted the measurements on a small pad at her desk.

"Scott is a good man." Rena lifted her arms so Opal could take the next measurement. "Life on a homestead is a lot quieter than life in town, but I'm adjusting."

"Hmm… I'm sure it is." Opal's attention was on the measurements more than the conversation. "Turn to your left, please." Opal shifted her tape. "Just one more."

Opal made several notes on her pad and slid the pencil back into place over her ear. She backed up to study Rena on the platform. "Would you please pivot to your right?" Opal twirled one finger in a counterclockwise circle. "Now to your left again, please."

"Do you have a particular pattern in mind?" Rena was becoming uncomfortable under Opal's scrutiny.

"Let's talk about it over a cup of tea."

A few minutes later they sat at a small table in the back corner of Opal's work area. Rena added sugar to her cup and stirred the rich liquid. "I've been cold through to the bone today. This is just what I needed."

"I'm glad to have a break from stitching. The hem I've been sewing seems never ending."

"Oh my. I guess some patterns call for a very full skirt."

"Yes, and some customers require a very full skirt." Opal winked at her over the top of her teacup.

Rena smiled. "Oh, you do have a fine sense of humor."

"Don't be fooled. There is truth in humor. The nugget of truth is what makes a thing funny." Opal's laughing eyes became serious. "But there are times when a seamstress knows that a truth is not a subject for humor."

Rena feared the woman knew her truth.

"Not to worry though. I've been a seamstress long enough to learn the practice of confidentiality."

She knew. Rena's measurements had revealed her truth.

Opal set her teacup on its saucer. "May I suggest some patterns for you that are versatile? There are some that will make up nicely but can be altered in the future." She cleared her throat. "If the need to take in a garment—or let it out—ever arose."

Relief flooded Rena. She was sure it showed on her face. "That is a splendid idea. Thank you for suggesting it." It occurred to Rena that Opal Pennington probably knew more secrets about the ladies in Gran Colina than anyone else in the county. She would thank the Lord above for her discretion when she prayed tonight before bed.

Scott finished his day at the jail and left Eli to watch the prisoner. He had hoped the judge would be able to come sooner than the middle of April. Six more weeks of guarding the accused killer would tax Scott and Eli more than they already were. He was glad for the help of several men who had volunteered to spend the night at the jail and give Scott and Eli a break.

The temperature seemed to be dropping. Flurries of snow floated on the wind as he stopped the wagon in front of Oscar's house. The front door opened, and Rena came out.

"Oh good. You're ready. I don't think this weather will get worse, but I would rather be at home than out in it."

"Me, too." She climbed up with his help. "I've been cold all day."

Scott urged the team forward, and they made short work of the trip home. "You hurry inside, while I take care of the animals and the barn chores."

By the time he was finished and entered the cabin, Rena had a fire going and supper ready to eat. He hung his jacket and went to stand in front of the fireplace. He rubbed his hands together. "You're spoiling me. It sure is nice to come home in the winter and have help."

She set two bowls of piping hot beans on the table and sat down. "It's freezing out there. I'm more than glad to work at the stove on a night like this."

After their supper, Scott waited until Rena settled into her chair with her Bible and stepped onto the front porch. He retrieved the partially finished cradle and brought it into the cabin. He set it on the rug in front of the hearth. Rena was so focused on her reading that she didn't notice it at first. When she looked up, her mouth dropped open, but she didn't say a word.

"Do you like it?"

In an instant, she was on her knees beside it running her hand along the curves of the wood. "Like it? It's perfect."

He laughed. "It's hardly perfect. It's not even finished. Be careful not to get a splinter." He pulled her hand away from the rough wood. I brought it inside so I can sand it in here where it's warm."

She looked up at him. "Will you put it in my room when you finish?" The hope in her eyes was all the thanks he could ever want for his labor.

"Of course." He realized he still held her hand. "The hard part is over. Only the fine work is left to do." He tugged her hand and pulled her to her feet. She withdrew from him and went back to her chair.

He knew her smile was for the coming child. The cradle gave tangible evidence of the baby's impending arrival.

Scott sanded the cradle as she read aloud from the Bible. Her voice was as soothing as the words she read. Until she turned to the Psalms.

"Except the Lord build the house, they labour in vain that build it—" He missed the next words she read as he wondered if that was what they were doing. Were they building their house, or was the Lord building it? Her voice drew him back. "Lo, children are an heritage of the Lord—" His mind refused to hear anything else she read tonight. All he heard was the screaming reality that the child she carried would be his sole heir. There would be no boy for him to name after himself. No girl who would carry his traits.

His inheritance from the Lord was another man's child.

The sanding of the cradle became more of a chore than a labor of love for a friend. He'd refused to take up anger against Rena for her actions, but tonight, in the warmth of the cozy cabin, the long-term consequences of their choices cried out to be heard. He'd built his home with every intention of marrying and raising a family to carry his name and tend his land for centuries to come. Louise's betrayal had killed that dream.

Tonight, he buried it in the sawdust at his feet, while he sanded off the rough edges of a cradle he'd built for the child of another man.

On Saturday, Scott drove Rena back into town. The weather had turned mild again, so they left directly after breakfast.

He kept his focus on the lane ahead of him. "What do you need to do in town?"

"I hope at least a portion of my clothes will be ready for me to pick up from Opal Pennington." She grabbed the front edge of the seat when one of the wagon wheels hit a hole in the lane, sliding them both forward. He instinctively put out a hand to steady her but released her arm as soon as she regained her balance. "I'd like to have one of the new outfits to wear to the Founder's Day celebration next Saturday."

"I have to attend a meeting this afternoon about the plans for the celebration." Since he'd shown her the cradle on Tuesday night, they hadn't had more than the most basic conversations. He blamed himself. She'd tried at first, but he hadn't responded well to her attempts at friendship.

He knew his behavior was unwarranted, but every time he worked on the cradle or caught a glimpse of her laying her hand on her growing abdomen, he fought against the pain of knowing he'd never have other children. He'd promised to provide for her child. And he would. He imagined he'd grow to love the baby, like he loved the children who attended Gran Colina Church.

But the part of him that longed to have a son to carry on his legacy ached with loss. He should have mourned this truth when Louise taught him the perils of love, but perhaps part of him had hoped beyond hope that the day would come when he'd be a husband and father.

Now he was a husband and father. But not in the true sense of either word.

Rena dragged him from his sad thoughts. "Who will be there?"

"Where?"

She turned to him with a wrinkled brow. "At the meeting."

"Oh." He pulled the reins to turn the team onto the main road that led into Gran Colina. "I'm sorry. My thoughts were wandering." Her countenance fell. She must imagine he'd rather think to himself than have a conversation with her. He couldn't keep pushing her away. Even if sometimes it wasn't an actual push, but merely aloofness, and only done to protect himself from more pain. "All the founders' family representatives."

"That should be an interesting gathering. My father in the room with Thomas Freeman. I wonder how a banker has time to run for mayor." She shook her head. "Then you and your deputy meeting Jack Jefferson."

He chuckled. "When you put it like that, the thought of any agreement by the end of the meeting is laughable. It's a wonder the town has survived these thirty years when the founders' descendants have come to reside on opposite sides of almost every issue."

"Are you supposed to be there to keep the peace?" She smiled at her remark.

"Your father asked me to come. He wants to make certain Eli and I are aware of all the plans in order to protect the townsfolk from anyone who's of a mind to become disorderly at the celebration. There's talk that Elmer Hicks wants to set up a booth in front of his place to sell spirits."

"That would be like inviting the rowdy atmosphere of the saloon into the street for the town's biggest event of the year. What about the women and children who don't want to be exposed to such?"

He nodded. "That's what we'll be deciding today."

"I hope you all make the right choices. The last thing Gran Colina needs before the election is another incident with drunken revelers."

"I don't disagree with you. I'm just not sure how Jefferson and Freeman will want to resolve this."

She huffed. "They'll want to allow it and then blame you and Papa if there's any trouble. Mark my words, when the judge comes they'll say the problems at the saloon weren't with the spirits but with you not being in town that night."

Rena was right. Jefferson hadn't missed an opportunity in the last two months to make Scott look incapable. Gilbert had been nearby, lurking and poised to emphasize any possible shortcomings in Scott.

In spite of all the tension he knew he'd face in the meeting today, he was relieved that he and Rena had been able to have a conversation where there had been smiles, and even laughter.

Tension in town was difficult. A marriage strained to the point of indifference was unbearable.

Lord, help us to recover the footing we built on mutual friendship. Help me to let go of the dreams that will never be. Guard my heart against bitterness to-

ward Rena. It would be unfair to make her uncomfortable and would only serve to make us both miserable.

Opal Pennington draped Rena's outfit across a small chair in the corner of her workroom. "I'm very pleased with how the fabric has done with this pattern." She pulled the curtain to separate the room from the front of her shop. "I can hardly wait to see it on you."

The rich brown material felt like a dream. Rena buttoned the top button of the short cape and twisted to see different angles of the outfit in the mirror. "It's lovely. The trim is perfect." She fingered the lacy, beige ribbon that lined the collar and the hem of the cape. "It fits beautifully."

"I made some adjustments here." Opal showed Rena the details of the waistband on the skirt. Special attention to the shape of the blouse especially pleased Rena. "This should serve you well."

"I think you're right. I look forward to wearing this next Saturday for the Founder's Day festivities." It would be nice to feel pretty again. After several weeks of squeamishness, followed by weeks of hard work on the homestead, and then having Scott withdraw from any sign of the friendship she'd come to rely on, Rena wanted to enjoy a day of fun. She missed the lighthearted days of visiting friends and leisure time. Not using the leisure wisely had been the reason for her isolation of late. She couldn't pinpoint the reason that Scott had put so much distance between them.

"I'm glad I was able to finish it in time." Opal

backed away and walked in a circle around Rena, inspecting every aspect of the garment. "The sheriff should be very pleased with your choice. You are very lovely."

"And you are too kind." Rena felt heat fill her face. It was natural for Opal to assume Rena would want to dress to please Scott. In recent days, he'd given Rena no hint of his approval over anything she'd done. "Do you have an idea of when the other garments will be done?"

"Would two weeks be soon enough?"

"Excellent." She unbuttoned the cape and admired the beige blouse she wore underneath. The same lace that adorned the cape accented the tiny pleats. "I'm very pleased with this particular outfit, and I look forward to seeing the others."

"I have some ideas on how to make them just as pretty."

Rena handed her the cape. "Do you have any remnants, or scraps that might be suitable for a project I'm working on? It's a small project. I thought I might try my hand at quilting."

Opal folded the cape and laid it aside. "I always have scraps. Do you have a particular color in mind?" She lined a box with tissue paper.

"A variety of pieces in complementary colors would be nice. Perhaps something in shades of green and yellow?" She didn't want to tell Opal why she wanted the fabric.

"I may have just the thing." Opal tapped her top lip

with her finger. "There are no large pieces, but since you are working on something small it may do."

"Wonderful."

"Would you say the finished project will be about this size?" Opal held her arms out to indicate the width.

Rena nodded. "I would say that is exactly right. I think you might be able to read my mind."

"Everyone needs a friend who understands their thoughts." Opal folded the brown skirt and laid it in the box. "I'll just finish up here and grab those remnants for you."

Rena stepped out of Opal's shop with the dress box tucked under one arm. In her other hand, she carried a bundle of beautiful remnants in soft shades of green and yellow with accents of pale blue. Opal had added a variety of ribbons for trim, wrapped the lot of it in brown paper and tied it with string. She'd even offered help should Rena run into trouble with the new quilt. In a few short months, her baby would sleep in the cradle that Scott had made beneath the quilt that she would begin to work on this very night.

She decided to drop by and visit with Charlotte for a few minutes, but first she'd leave her parcels at Scott's office.

Just as she climbed the steps to enter, Betty Alexander came out of the post office across the street. "Oh, Rena!" She was waving a paper in her hand. "Just a moment, please." A freight wagon passed on the street between them, and then Betty crossed to her. "I want to show you this."

"What is it?"

"I've just seen this article in the Dallas paper. A ship went down off the coast of California. Little more than a month ago." Betty was pointing at a picture of a boat leaving a harbor. "The article says it was on the way to Alaska but sank before it got into deep water. There were no survivors."

Rena's insides knotted. Eugene was most likely on that ship. But why would Betty be bringing this to her attention? "That is tragic news."

Betty offered the paper to Rena, but she shook her head. "I don't wish to read the details."

Betty frowned. "Aren't you the least bit curious?" Betty pursed her lips. "Do you think that's the ship Eugene Rodgers was on?"

Rena caught her breath. Betty was connecting her to Eugene. "I'm sure I don't know."

"Really? You haven't a clue?" The woman nodded in a most irritating way. "You know, Rena, you learn a lot about people working in the post office. Many of the people who come in take their mail and read it at home. They choose to savor the news it brings in private. Some just rip their letters right open and read them in front of me." She leaned in close. "I do hear the most personal stories at those times."

"I'm sure you do." Rena forced a smile. "If you'll excuse me, I have some things to attend to."

As if Rena hadn't said a word, Betty continued. "Postcards are the most interesting though. There was the time Mrs. Jefferson's aunt from Philadelphia sent a lovely card with a picture of the Liberty Bell. And the one from New York City that came last Christmas to

Reverend Gillis." She lifted a finger. "But you know what many folks don't think about? Those postcards have the message right there on the outside for all the world to read." Her eyes narrowed. "It's not necessary for a person handling the mail to pry into the business of the person to whom the mail is addressed. It's almost impossible not to see the message when looking for the information needed to deliver the mail. Why, those words can seem to jump off the card. Especially when the postcard comes from far away and boasts a unique picture on the front. Say, a picture of a famous landmark—like the Liberty Bell—or a city like New York." She lowered her voice. "Or a city on the coast of somewhere like California."

Rena could feel the blood leaving her face as she remembered the postcard from Eugene. Would this woman stand on the sidewalk in front of her husband's office and try to cast aspersions on Rena's past association with a man who was most likely dead? There was no way Betty had any knowledge of Rena's connection to Eugene. All she had seen was a postcard.

Lord, give me wisdom.

"What are you trying to say, Betty?"

The office door opened behind her, and Scott stepped outside. "Hello, ladies. You look deep in discussion. Is anything wrong?" He looked at Betty first, but his gaze landed on Rena and stayed there.

They'd promised each other the truth.

"Betty has a newspaper article with a story about a ship going down off the coast of California while on the way to Alaska. All the passengers perished.

She has asked if I think Eugene Rodgers was one of the passengers." Betty's smile resembled a sneer, as though she was gaining satisfaction with what she believed was Rena's discomfort. "I've told her that I don't know, but she's curious because she read a postcard sent to me by Mr. Rodgers that said he was leaving for Alaska."

Rena hated that Scott was forced into the middle of such a discussion. If dealing with hints of her past felt like this, how would her heart survive if word of her baby's parentage was ever exposed?

How would Scott deal with it now? On the street in front of his office.

Chapter Nine

So Rena was face-to-face with the past she'd given her freedom to conceal. The strain on her features was what brought Scott outside. He'd watched from his desk as she'd grown more and more tense each time Betty spoke. He appreciated that Rena had chosen to deal with the conversation honestly and would do his best to help her. They might not be on the friendliest of terms, but he would not let anyone taunt her.

"I see. That must be the postcard you told me about." He turned back to Betty. "I was unaware that reading the contents of someone's mail was part of your job."

Betty looked taken aback. "I merely sought to make your wife aware that someone of her recent acquaintance has likely been killed in a terrible tragedy. Death is such an awful thing. Especially when it strikes a close associate."

Scott nodded in agreement. "I am sorry for the man's death. It is never welcome news to hear of someone's passing. Allow me to thank you for your concern and assure you that, though my wife—like many of the people in Gran Colina—was acquainted with Mr. Rodgers, they are not close associates."

"Really?" Betty asked Rena. "I wonder because no one else received any communication from him after he left Gran Colina. I gathered you must have shared some sort of closeness. The postcard did come before any association between the two of you—" she pointed at Scott and Rena "—was known. I drew a likely conclusion. Why else would a man write to a young woman?"

This had gone on long enough. Rena's blank expression was frozen on her face, but he knew it could give way to her true concern at any moment. He had to squelch Betty's curiosity and get his wife off the sidewalk. He could think of no better way than to turn the focus onto Betty. "You pay a great deal of attention to the mail that comes through your office."

"I do." She was bold in her response. "I take great pride in my work. It's my duty to gather and deliver the mail with the utmost attention to detail."

He grunted. "How many people are aware of the level of inquisitiveness you deploy in your duties?"

"Excuse me? Are you suggesting impropriety on my part?"

"I am suggesting that it is not prudent to draw conclusions about a matter based on the vague scrawling of a postcard. Unless you'd like to give the impression to me or the people of Gran Colina that you use your position to gather information that you spread at will, regardless of whether the information is founded in truth." He took Rena's arm. "If you'll excuse us." He opened his office door and held it for Rena to enter.

Betty let out a huff and stomped down the steps. She was halfway across the street when he closed the door and turned to see Rena dissolving into tears.

Eli Gardner jumped up from his chair across the room. "What's happened?"

Scott waved him off and wrapped Rena in his arms. He'd kept his distance from her emotionally and physically, but he didn't have it in him to let her stand there and cry without comfort.

She sobbed against his shirt. He couldn't make out the words, but it sounded like she wanted to go across the street and tell Betty Alexander a thing or two.

"It'll be okay, Rena." He patted her hair with one hand. It was as soft as it was shiny. The fresh scent of flowers drifted to him. He'd refused to allow himself to think about her beauty, but holding her close brought every detail into focus. She fit under his chin like a hand in a glove. He stilled his hand on her hair and held her while she raged against her pain.

Eli pushed his hat onto his head and gave Scott a parting salute. The door closed behind him.

Rena caught her breath and clung to Scott. Her words were muffled against his chest but discernable. "She was awful. How could she say those things to me?"

Without forethought, he dropped a kiss on the top of her head. It was a subconscious gesture meant to console. It might console Rena, but it unsettled something in the core of Scott's being. And left him changed. He'd been compassionate for Rena and her pain before he'd taken her in his arms, but now he felt that pain. The hurt she endured crept into his soul and refused to be denied. The depth of it tormented him and cried out to be relieved.

"Rena, we can't fret about what she thinks or says. She is a busybody. I didn't realize how much of one until today, but now we know."

She jerked her head up and dashed away the tears. "You are right. And that makes her words pointless. I will not cry over them." She sniffed and withdrew from his embrace. He let her go but didn't release the comfort it had been to have her in his arms. He'd intended to comfort her, but her closeness moved him.

He dragged the fingers of both hands through his hair. "That's the attitude to take. Don't let her win. Not Betty or Cyrus, or anyone else who may try to stir up controversy."

She gave a curt nod. "Ignore her. And her assumptions. That is what I'll do."

"Ignoring what people say about you won't keep you out of trouble." The words came from the man in the cell.

Scott and Rena turned to look at him. Scott didn't like Rena being here with the man, but there had been nothing else to do for her at the moment but bring her inside. He'd completely forgotten the man was there until he spoke.

"This conversation does not concern you, Vernon."

"Since you're having it right in front of me, I can

hardly avoid it." Vernon Ramsey shrugged. "It's not easy when people who don't know you try to control your destiny. I'm sitting here, facing a noose, because no one will believe me when I say Gordon Dixon was going to shoot me. Had even pulled his gun first." The man's voice rose in anger. Anger that came in waves over the last few weeks.

Rena looked at Scott. He could see her mind working and knew she wanted him to find some way to prove the man's innocence. Only, Scott didn't know if he was innocent. He wanted her to understand how complicated it was, and he wanted Vernon to know he'd investigated the case from every conceivable angle.

"We've been over this, and there's no one to back up your story. You've confessed to the killing. It's in the hands of the judge and jury. There's nothing more for me to do."

"Why would I confess to killing him if I thought it wasn't in self-defense? I could have hid my gun and pointed to someone else as the culprit." He clung to the bars as if he could shake them loose the way Samson had pushed down the pillars of the temple in the Bible.

"What about—" Rena paused when Scott held up his hand, but only for a moment. "I was just going to say, what if someone else listened to the story? I know you've been over the details many times, but maybe a fresh telling will give a new clue." Her eyes lit up. He marveled that within minutes of being the target of hateful gossip, she was at the ready to fight someone else's battle. This was the energetic young woman he'd known for two years. She settled on a chair in front of the cell. "Besides, it will give me something to think about while you're meeting with the town founders."

Scott checked his watch. "I have one hour. Not a minute more." He glared at Vernon. "Not one bit of trouble out of you, or it'll be the last mercy you get from me."

Vernon nodded and sat on his bunk on the far wall of the cell. He faced Rena with every appearance of patience.

"Do you have some paper, Scott? I want to make notes." Rena spent the next hour quizzing Vernon Ramsey about how he came to be in Gran Colina, how he knew Gordon Dixon—the man he'd shot— and who among the saloon goers could have seen the gun he claimed Mr. Dixon held on him.

Because he'd only arrived in town hours before the shooting, Vernon didn't know the names of the locals. Rena jotted down the descriptions he gave her. "What about anyone behind you at the saloon?"

Vernon held out his hands, palms up. "That's just it. I couldn't see who was behind me. Even if I could have, I wouldn't know who to take at their word. It's like I told you, Sheriff. I only heard voices. A couple of them I'd recognize if I heard them again, but what's the use of trying when I don't know folks. One man was particularly annoying. Kept taunting Gordon. It was just saloon talk. You know the kind I mean. Boasting, aggravating bluster for the most part."

The door opened and Eli stuck his head in the office. Scott motioned for him to enter. "I'm glad you're back. I've got to leave." Scott stood and pulled Rena's cape from the hall tree by the door. "The meeting begins in ten minutes. I think you've asked enough questions for one day."

"There is a lot here to check into." Rena folded the paper and slid it into her reticule. She let Scott arrange her cape on her shoulders. "We can talk about it over supper tonight."

"I don't want you to settle your hopes on any of this making a difference." Scott noted the hope in her face. "You either."

Vernon acknowledged his caution with a nod. "I appreciate your interest just the same, Mrs. Braden. It's nice to know that someone cared enough to try and clear my name."

"I've needed the help of others myself." Rena walked to the cell and wrapped her fingers around one of the bars. "I'd like to think that someone would come to my aid if I were in your situation. It's easy for folks to judge others guilty without knowing their situation." The pain in her voice rang with truth, and it hurt Scott that she spoke from experience.

But Vernon Ramsey had shot a man. He wasn't in the jail for a trivial matter.

"Rena, it's time to go."

Rena visited with Charlotte while Scott met with the descendants of the founders of Gran Colina. They sat on the settee in the family residence at Green's Grand Hotel. Charlotte curled up in one corner with her feet tucked under her. Rena sat on the opposite end with a cup of tea.

"I had a new dress made." Rena took another cookie from the plate on the tray between them. "It's a lovely shade of brown. I'm going to wear it on Founder's Day."

"How wonderful for you! So many nice things happening. A new husband, a homestead and new clothes. When will I ever have such joys of my own?" She stuck out her lips in an exaggerated pout, but her laughter spoiled her attempt to appear jealous.

"Every man in the county will attend the festivities next weekend."

"If I'm left taking care of Sarah and Michael, I won't even have time to join in the fun."

"You know you love those two."

"I do." Charlotte reached for a cookie. "Having a little brother and sister can be wonderful and a lot of work at the same time. They're so young. At five and six, they want to play and explore. They are sweet, but is it so wrong to want children of my own?"

"No, it's not. It's best to wait until the right man comes along. You'll see. It'll happen for you."

"I'm going to listen to you." Charlotte grinned. "You've set a fine example for me to follow. I'm going to aim for the kind of happiness you have."

Rena cringed at the words. She wanted to encourage Charlotte without being dishonest. "It's best to pray for God to guide you. You'll have your own special happiness one day. I'm certain it will be beyond all your dreams." Rena picked up another cookie. "Did you make these?"

"Yes. Momma is determined to make a baker out of me. It's probably my favorite part of working here."

"These are delicious."

"Do you make sweets for Scott?"

"Sometimes. I made tea cakes the other day, and they turned out good. The truth is that Scott will eat almost anything."

Charlotte went to stare out the front window. "What's it like, Rena? Being married?"

The question wasn't unexpected, but Rena chose her words with care. She did not want to deceive Charlotte or cause her friend to let go of her dreams just because Rena's life had not turned out the way they both imagined. "Scott is a good man. He takes good care of me. I consider myself blessed."

"Are you happy?" Charlotte came back to sit across from her. "You never say. You look wonderful, so I have to think that glow about you is the result of utter happiness."

"Oh, Charlotte, you are a poetic soul. Yes, I have a good life." It was true. Many things in her life were much better than she deserved. "I am happy."

A shadow crossed the front window, and a knock sounded at the front door of the residence.

"Oh, I'm so disappointed. The afternoon has just flown by, and here's Scott to take you away again." Charlotte went to open the door.

Rena stood and brushed cookie crumbs from her

skirt. When she lifted her head, she could see the tension in Scott.

"Hello, Charlotte. I'm sorry to burst in and leave so quickly, but Rena and I have some business to attend to."

"Thank you for the visit." Rena gave her friend a hug and followed Scott outside. As soon as the door closed behind them, she asked, "What's the matter?"

"The meeting was as harmonious as you could expect. No one agreed on anything. As it stands, everyone is going to do exactly what they did last year. They refused to listen to new ideas. Instead of the normal speeches from the mayor and the preacher, Jefferson insisted on giving Thomas Freeman and Gilbert an opportunity to speak to the crowds."

"So the celebration of the founding of the town has now become a political rally?"

"Your father and I tried to get them to see that, but it was pointless. With all the uproar that Jefferson has created in the last few weeks, you'd think they would want to have a celebration that was peaceful and without commotion."

They were walking toward Scott's office at a pace that had Rena struggling to keep up. She stopped on the street. Scott had taken several strides before he realized she was no longer beside him. He turned and held his hands out. "Are you coming?"

She walked at her normal speed. When she caught up to him, she put a hand on his arm. The muscle beneath her hand tightened. "Were you and my father the only ones opposed to their suggestions?"

"What difference does that make?"

"You and Papa represent everyone in Gran Colina. Even the ornery children of the founders." She grinned up at him, hoping to alleviate his stress. "If Thomas Freeman and Gilbert Jefferson were the mayor and the sheriff, and you and Papa were running as their opponents in the election, you would probably think that the Founder's Day festivities were a perfect opportunity to share your reasons with the townsfolk. I don't think it's an unreasonable suggestion."

"Well, that's just fine." Scott took a step back. "My own wife wants to give my opposition a voice."

"Your opposition has a voice. As much as I don't want to hear a thing they have to say, this is Texas, and the fair election requires a fair hearing of all the candidates." She had a thought. "What if you set aside a separate day for a political rally? Then no one could complain. You and Papa could pledge that you would not use Founder's Day for political speeches. The people of Gran Colina can enjoy their celebration of the town and founding families, and they can also hear the views of the people who want to lead the town. Surely no one could find fault with such a plan."

He pondered what she'd said, and while he did, she studied the way his bottom lip lifted up on the left side of his mouth. His blue eyes were clear, yet narrowed as he thought. She wanted to brush the unruly hair from his forehead and tell him not to frown. Instead, she found herself captivated by his gaze. Drawn to him by some unseen force that held her frozen in time.

"Hey, Sheriff, look out!" Russell Henderson pulled

on the reins of his team in an effort to turn his wagon. Scott scooped Rena out of the path of the coming horses.

"You young married folks don't need to stand in the middle of the street gawking at one another. Somebody could get hurt." Russell waved and drove the wagon around them.

"Are you hurt?" Scott put his hands on her shoulders and quickly moved them to her elbows.

It took great effort to catch her breath and not let Scott see how he had affected her. "No, I'm fine." She straightened her cape. "I think he was right. We need to get out of the street."

He cupped her elbow with his hand and led her up the steps to his office. "I think you may have just solved our problem. I have to work for a few minutes, but on our way out of town, I'd like to stop by and speak to the men who were at the meeting and recommend a separate rally."

The realization that she had been able to help him brought a deep satisfaction. She hoped it was only the first of many times that she would prove her worth to him.

Chapter Ten

Founder's Day dawned clear and mild. Scott did the morning chores and loaded the wagon with the food Rena had prepared for the picnic. He leaned against the wheel and waited for her to come out of the house. He adjusted his hat lower on his brow, and the front door opened.

His breath caught in his throat when Rena stopped on the porch. She brushed the front of her skirt with one hand and stilled when she looked up at him. Her shoulders lifted in inquiry. This strong woman who'd stood toe-to-toe with his prisoner was questioning her appearance.

He took off his hat and gave a swooping bow. "Ma'am, would you do me the honor of accompanying me to the Founder's Day festivities in Gran Colina?"

She giggled but didn't move from her spot. "Why, kind sir, that is a generous offer, but I am not certain of your motivation. Do you wish to merely escort me into town and leave me to my own devices, or will you be enjoying the events of the day at my side?" Even in the shadow of the porch, he could see her blush. She was flirting with him.

He approached the steps. "My intention would be to spend the day with you, but as pretty as you look, I'm sure to have to guard you against others in pursuit of your company." He winked and held out a hand to her.

"I'd be delighted to spend the day with you, Sheriff Braden." She slid her hand into his and descended the steps.

Rena looked down at him after he helped her into the wagon. "Thank you for making me laugh."

"We're both due for some lighthearted fun. What do you say we make the most of today?" He went to the other side of the wagon and climbed aboard. Lifting the reins, he glanced sideways at her. "You look lovely today."

"Thank you for saying so. And thank you for all my new clothes." She adjusted her cape. "This is the first outfit. Opal said the other outfits should be completed soon."

"I'm happy that you're pleased."

Scott drove them into town then. They were early, but the streets were already busy. The festivities were soon to begin when they met up with Oscar.

"Good morning, Rena." Her father kissed her on the cheek. "You're looking especially lovely today."

"I have to agree with you." Scott shook hands with his father-in-law. "I see they finished building the platform."

Rena looked around at the growing crowd. "I'm

so glad you were able to work out having a political rally next Saturday afternoon. Hopefully everyone can enjoy today."

Her father nodded in agreement. "I'd like to take the two of you to supper at the hotel after the rally next week. I want to celebrate your birthday, Rena."

Scott had no idea it would be her birthday.

"Papa, you don't have to do that. I don't need a celebration this year."

"You may be a grown and married woman now, but you'll always be my baby girl. You can count on me celebrating your birthday every year. Your momma and I agreed that, after our wedding day, the day you were born was the best day of our lives."

"Oh, Papa. That may be the sweetest thing you've ever said to me." She looked at Scott. "Would it be okay with you to have dinner next Saturday?"

"Of course. I look forward to it." Her birthday would be the perfect time to give her the wedding ring he wanted to buy.

Opal Pennington approached Rena. "Mrs. Braden, you look very pretty today." She grinned. "If it's okay for me to say so."

"Thank you, Opal." Rena darted a glance at Scott. "I feel pretty today."

Oscar pulled his watch from his vest pocket and opened it. He tapped the glass. "It's almost time to get started. I'm going to go to the platform and make sure everyone is ready."

Scott offered his arm to Rena, and she slipped her

hand inside his elbow. "Ladies, shall we join the mayor for the opening ceremonies?"

Oscar led the opening with his usual aplomb. As arranged, someone from each of the founding families greeted those who had gathered to celebrate the founding of Gran Colina. In his capacity as mayor, Oscar made the introductions. Jack Jefferson went first, lauding his father's initiative in helping to establish the town. Eli Gardner gave a more humble appreciation of his father's role. Oscar spoke last.

He held out a hand toward Jack and Eli on the platform beside him. "Our fathers had no idea when they joined forces to create this great town, what a magnificent place it would become. They started with three families, and today we're a thriving community that has grown to include all the successful businesses you see around you. I don't imagine one of our fathers would have known what to think if you told them the railroad would even build a station here. The Good Lord has blessed us. Now let the celebrating begin."

A cheer went up from the crowd, and folks dispersed to take part in the games and events that were scheduled to fill the day.

Scott and Rena agreed to start at the refreshment booth in front of Green's Grand Hotel.

"Isn't this exciting?" Charlotte used a ladle to dip lemonade into small cups. "I think everyone in the county is here today."

"You're probably right." Rena accepted a tea cake and a cup of lemonade.

Scott paid for their refreshments and wrapped a

tea cake in a napkin and tucked it in the pocket of his shirt for later. "Your booth is sure to be a success."

Rena nodded and made a humming sound. "These are delicious. I keep practicing, but I can't figure out your mother's secret ingredient."

"Take another for later." Charlotte pointed at the platter of tea cakes. "I'm glad you're eating again. For a few weeks there, I was concerned you might waste away to nothing."

Scott watched Rena's attempt not to overreact to Charlotte's observation. "I think married life agrees with her."

Rena choked on her lemonade, and he had to pat her on the back to stop her coughing. "Really, Scott! You're embarrassing me." She protested, but her smile gave Charlotte the impression that he was speaking the truth. He'd made the statement in an effort to continue their public affirmation of their relationship. Her response pricked at his heart.

As much as he never thought it would happen, Scott was growing to care for Rena. Two months of friendship and close association had endeared her to him. He must be careful. Rena had agreed to their marriage for the sake of her child. She had given him no reason to believe she would ever expect—or want—more from him.

The preacher and his wife joined them. "This is always such fun." Mrs. Gillis asked Charlotte for a cup of lemonade. "What is your favorite event, Rena?"

"There are so many it's difficult to choose." Rena thought for a moment. "Maybe horseshoes. I always laugh at how the men argue and boast over such a thing as tossing a horseshoe through the air."

"Will you be trying your hand at that today, Preacher?" Scott planned to compete.

Reverend Gillis shook his head. "I've been asked to make sure the scoring is done fairly. It seems that some of the competitors tried to improve their scores last year while no one was looking."

They all laughed and moved away to other things.

A few minutes later, Scott took his place on the sidelines for the beginning of the horse races. The men who wanted to compete would complete a circuit mapped out at the edge of town, with the start/finish line in front of Henderson's Livery.

He gave the instructions. "Gentlemen, there are men posted at four points along the route. You must retrieve a flag at every point and bring the flag back with you to this spot. The first three people to complete the race with all four flags will be awarded ribbons."

Gilbert Jefferson's horse edged out in front of the others. "Back in line, Jefferson!" Eli Gardner shouted from the opposite end of the starting line of horses.

The riders were as varied a group as any Scott had seen. Charles Green, the hotel owner, was lined up next to the saloon owner. The barber, Alfred Murray, rode a mare he'd rented from Henderson's Livery. Thomas Freeman had decided at the last minute to participate.

Scott stepped forward and raised his gun into the air. "On the count of three, I will fire the starting shot."

The riders pulled the reins tight in preparation.

"One, two, three." Scott pulled the trigger on the last word, and the horses bolted.

Laughter erupted in the crowd of bystanders as Alfred's horse reared up on his hind legs and dropped the man in the dust left by the other horses. One horse made a sharp right turn and left the planned course, no doubt headed for home. The rest of the group fanned out as they left the sight of the spectators.

Rena put a hand on his arm. "How long do you think it will take?"

"Not more than ten minutes for the winners." Scott pointed after the horse galloping off on his own. "I'm not sure that one will return at all." He grinned at her. "Do you like this event?"

She watched the horizon for returning riders, though they both knew no one would come yet. "I enjoy seeing the men come together to spur one another on in sport." She nodded toward the women and children who waited with them. "I think healthy competition is a good way to teach life lessons. These young boys will watch their fathers, and then grow up to race as their own children watch in years to come. It's part of our history. Something that pulls us together as a community."

"This town is important to you, isn't it?" Her love for her father had been obvious to him. True concern for the town had been secondary.

"It's all I've ever known. These people, the life we have here." She gazed into the distance. "Once

I thought I might like to travel and see more of the world. Not anymore." Her voice faded with each word.

He leaned in so no one else would hear. "Don't let all of your dreams fade, Rena."

"They didn't fade away, Scott." She looked him in the eye. "I killed them."

Shouts of excitement roared through the street. "Here they come!"

Rena clapped and cheered with everyone else as Doc Taylor raced across the finish line with four red flags in hand.

"Well done, Doc!" Oscar congratulated the oldest man to attempt the race. "You've taught those young ones a lesson about horsemanship." He pointed at the coming riders. "Think they'll make it back before dark?"

Laughter and cheers grew to screams of excitement as the next four riders approached. They ran neck and neck. Gilbert Jefferson was on the outside trying to nose by Charles Green. Jack Jefferson pushed through the middle of the pack, but Thomas Freeman edged out in front and took second place. Charles Green's horse stumbled when Jack Jefferson turned his horse against him, and Gilbert came in third.

Each rider pulled hard on the reins to stop their mounts.

"Whoa!" Charles slid out of the saddle and onto one knee to check the front leg of his horse. He found that the animal had suffered an abrasion but no broken bones. He bolted to Jack Jefferson's horse and grabbed the halter.

"Let go." Jefferson pulled the horse in the opposite direction.

"You come down here and tell me what you were thinking." He pointed to his horse. "You could have caused me to have to put him down. All for a second place ribbon?"

"Are you calling me a cheater?"

Scott stepped up as Jefferson dismounted. "Men, let's calm down."

"You saw him, Sheriff! He deliberately ran into my horse." Charles never carried on in such a way, but Scott had seen what Charles saw.

"I saw the horses collide."

"I don't cotton to being accused." Jack Jefferson leveled a stare at Charles.

"And I don't cotton to my horse being injured." Charles was no longer shouting, but he was just as upset.

Scott wanted this to end peacefully and soon. "Charles, how bad is your horse injured?"

"It's a flesh wound. But that's not the point."

Jack Jefferson inspected the feet of his horse. "Why would I put my mount at risk?"

"Hey, fellas." Oscar bellowed from the finish line. "Let's pass out these ribbons and get on to the next competition."

Scott looked at Charles. "Do you think your horse will be okay?" Charles nodded. "Are you willing to let this go then?"

Charles narrowed his eyes on Jack Jefferson. "If he stays out of my way."

"Jefferson, what about you?" Scott knew if he didn't ask both men, Jefferson would take offense. "Can we accept the results of the race and move on?"

"I've got no problem. Never did." He climbed into the saddle.

Scott put a hand on Charles's shoulder when he bristled at Jefferson's remark. "I've got some ribbons to hand out. I trust the two of you will give each other a wide berth for the rest of the day."

"It's not me you have to worry about. I'm not a troublemaker." Charles took his horse by the reins and led him away.

Scott handed out the ribbons, and everyone headed to the church for the picnic lunch.

Rena walked beside him. "I hope you're hungry. I made buttermilk pie."

"You did?" He tucked his hand under her elbow. "That sounds like just the thing."

"Maybe we'll make it through lunch without anyone needing the services of the sheriff." Her laughter lifted his spirits. This was his third Founder's Day celebration in Gran Colina. Having Rena by his side had already made it his favorite.

"Wake up, sleepyhead." Rena pushed on Scott's shoulder. He'd tucked his jacket under his head, covered his face with his hat and gone into a deep sleep.

Scott slid his hat back. "How is a man supposed to function on a full belly?"

"People are almost ready to play horseshoes. You

spread the quilt so close to where they set it up that you could get thumped on the head."

The men who intended to play horseshoes began to gather.

"I'll put the picnic things in the wagon and come back to play." Scott picked up the basket with the remnants of their food, and she handed him the quilt.

"I'll be right here." Rena found a spot where she would have a good view of the competition.

Louise Freeman came to stand beside her. "You and Scott seem very happy."

Rena had never been on friendly terms with Louise. She hoped Louise would walk away before Scott returned. It could be awkward for him to find his wife conversing with his former fiancée. "We are happy." She saw Thomas Freeman motion for his wife to join him a few yards away.

Louise waved in response with the imported lace gloves she held in one hand. "I hope Scott knows that Thomas running for mayor has nothing to do with our—" she cleared her throat "—history."

The woman had not looked Rena in the eye during the entire exchange. The overly sweet, thinly disguised feelings of superiority grated on Rena.

"I'm sure the Good Lord knows your husband's motives. Just as He knows the motives of my husband and father." Rena pivoted to stand in front of Louise, forcing a face-to-face interaction. "My prayer is that the good people of Gran Colina come to know those motives, as well."

"Are you suggesting that Thomas's motives are anything but altruistic?" Louise's countenance paled.

"I'm saying plainly that your husband has a habit of pursuing things that belong to others."

Louise attempted to fan herself with her flimsy gloves. "How dare you speak to me in such a manner?" People began to stare when she raised her voice.

Thomas came to see what had upset his wife. He put an arm around her shoulders. "Are you okay, my dear? Has something happened?"

"The sheriff's wife has insulted me. She insulted you, too." She gasped for air as if no one had ever forced her to face a truth.

"What have you said to her?" Thomas glared at Rena.

Louise let out a squeak that made Rena laugh. "You said—" She closed her mouth as if it only just occurred to her that she could not repeat Rena's remarks. To do so would intimate that Thomas had pursued Louise while she was engaged to be married to Scott.

Thomas refused to be satisfied. "What did she say?"

Rena answered for her. "Nothing has happened, other than the fact that I have called into question your motive for running for the office of mayor. I believe you are seeking my father's position and ultimately Scott's removal from office by virtue of your support of Gilbert Jefferson's candidacy."

"You have no right to say such things to my wife."

Scott spoke from behind Rena. "And you will not speak to my wife in that way." Concern and anger warred on his face when he looked at her. "What is going on here?"

"Your wife has insulted my wife and called my integrity into question in the middle of the celebration designed to celebrate the great town of Gran Colina." Thomas puffed out his chest. "My understanding was that today would be void of political remarks. It appears to me—" he stretched one arm wide to indicate the listening bystanders "—that you, Sheriff Braden, need to control your wife."

Rena pinned the banker with her stare. "I am not a barn animal to be controlled." Several of the women nearby laughed.

"When your husband holds political office, you should control yourself. If you don't, he owes it to the town who pays his keep to prevent you from causing a disturbance as you have done today." Thomas barely hid the sneer that threatened to expose the depth of his displeasure.

"This disturbance began when your wife approached me."

Louise denied her part in the matter. "I did nothing to justify your reaction."

Scott held up a hand. "I've heard enough. And so has everyone else standing here. We may all disagree on a lot of things, but I know we can all agree that we came here today to celebrate Gran Colina. Let's do that."

"Hear, hear." Papa pushed through the crowd. "If you folks will make room, we'll see if someone besides Alfred Murray or Eli Gardner can win the horseshoe competition this year." Her father encouraged the people to join him in watching the games and headed back the way he'd come.

Thomas and Louise Freeman walked away, and Scott put a hand on her shoulder. Rena cringed inside as she caught different ones turning for a glimpse of her and Scott. Some whispered, and some shook their heads. What had she done? She had jeopardized everything she and Scott were working to accomplish. Shame consumed her.

When it became apparent that several people were reluctant to turn their attention back to the events of the day, Scott asked her to take a walk with him.

Once they were out of earshot of the others, he said, "I don't know how all of that got started, but it's exactly what we don't need."

"I'm so sorry. She was just so arrogant."

"What could she possibly have said to upset you like that?"

Rena remembered the entire conversation. "I should have heeded your wisdom. You were right. Sometimes it is hard to be slow to speak."

She didn't know how much damage her outburst had caused. Whatever the toll, she had no one to blame but herself. Once again, others would likely bear the cost of her actions.

"That is one of the hardest verses in the Bible." They had walked as far as their wagon. "Would you like to sit for a while?"

"Yes." Before she realized what he intended, he'd

picked her up by the waist. She grasped his shoulders and held on as he set her on the back of the wagon.

He climbed up beside her. "I have a confession to make."

"What?" She couldn't imagine anything he'd need to confess.

"I heard that conversation." He nodded in the direction of the crowd watching the games.

"What? How?" Rena played her words over in her mind. Had she said anything she wouldn't have wanted him to hear?

"I was standing there." He indicated a tree between the wagon and the spot where they'd eaten their lunch. "Louise had just walked up to you when I stopped there."

"Why didn't you let me know you were there?"

"At first, I just didn't want to have to make small talk with Louise. I've done a good job of avoiding her most of the last year. I saw no need for today to be any different."

"Do you still care for her?" It wasn't fair to ask, but if he was keeping his distance because of lingering emotions, Rena thought she should know it.

"No." His tone was emphatic. "I put her in my past the day she left me for another man."

They sat silent for a minute. "I'm glad. For your sake. It would be cruel for you to pine for someone like that."

"I was hurt when she married Thomas Freeman, but that was a long time ago." He swung one boot in a slow rhythm. "There's no need to let the past ruin the present." He caught her eye. "Or the future."

"How did you get so smart, Scott Braden?" He was wiser than men twice his age.

"Painful lessons are excellent teachers."

"I'm sorry I made such a fuss."

He put his hands behind him and leaned back. "Wonder what we should do about it?"

She giggled. "You could beat him up."

"I could." A smile tugged at the corner of his mouth. She was captivated again by the way his bottom lip pulled up in an almost-perpetual grin. "Do you think I'd get more votes next month if I did?"

"Maybe." She sobered. "I need to apologize. To both of them." She hung her head and hated the idea of doing it, but it was the right thing to do."

"Want to wait until they finish with the horseshoes?"

"Please." She left him on the wagon and walked in the churchyard, praying for the right words and the strength to say them.

Before the games ended, Rena made her way to the edge of the gathering. When her father was about to pronounce the winner, she caught his attention.

"I need to speak to you for a minute."

He leaned close, and she whispered to him. He nodded and addressed the group. "Before I pass out the ribbons for this event, my daughter would like to say something." She stepped up beside him. "Go ahead, Rena."

"Haven't you said enough?" The call from the back of the group sounded like it came from Jack Jefferson.

She swallowed and squared her shoulders. "You're right." Murmurs rippled through the air. "Well, mostly right. I've actually said too much today. I spoke unkindly to Mr. and Mrs. Freeman. I did so in a public manner, and it was wrong." She found Thomas and Louise in the mix of people. "I'm asking for you to forgive me." She cleared her throat. "I promise to do my best to prevent such a display in the future."

The audience had been captivated by her speech. Now they turned to see the reaction of Thomas and Louise. Rena caught sight of Scott standing at the back of the group. He stood taller than many of the men there. She vowed to herself in that moment never to bring shame on him again. She'd rather bite her tongue than suffer the humiliation she felt while she waited for the Freemans to respond.

Thomas lifted a hand to the crowd. "Mrs. Braden, we accept your apology, and, in the spirit of the festivities of the day, we hope we can all put aside anything that has put a damper on the celebration."

She thanked him and stepped aside for her father to award the prizes for the games. She would have wandered back to the wagon, but Scott intercepted her.

"Going off to lick your wounds?" His tone was kind, but she hated the truth of his words.

She nodded.

"Don't." A roar of laughter went up from the crowd behind her. "Everyone else is having a fun afternoon. You've done more to correct this situation than anyone I know would have done. Let it go. Enjoy the rest of the day with me."

"I'm embarrassed." She stared at the ground between them.

He ducked so he could see her face. "'A merry heart doeth good like a medicine.' If we do something fun, you'll feel better."

Scott reached for her hand.

Rena shook her head. "Why did you marry someone—me—when you knew there would be times that I'd do things without thinking? I don't mean to, but I attract trouble."

With a growing smile, he held his hand out until she put hers in it. His fingers closed around hers. "I'm a man who likes a challenge."

"May God help you. I don't know that you'll ever encounter a bigger challenge than me."

Chapter Eleven

Darkness settled in as Scott finished walking the perimeter of the grassy field that surrounded Jack Jefferson's barn. Jefferson's ranch was close to town and boasted the largest barn in the county. During one of their contentious planning meetings, Jefferson had suggested that his wife would like to host the dance there. In spite of Scott's personal differences with Jefferson, it was a good choice for the end of the Founder's Day festivities. He hoped this check to insure that nothing was amiss on the property might be the last of his sheriff's duties for the night.

Scott was pleased they had made it through the day with no trouble at the saloon. People had engaged in all of the planned activities, and by dusk, a jolly mood settled over the town. He prayed that nothing would hinder the rest of the celebration.

Eli Gardner was making a round of the town businesses before going on duty at the jail. If things went as Scott hoped, he and Rena could take part in the first couple of dances, and then head for home.

The lively strains of violin music spilled out of the open barn doors and filled the night. Scott stepped inside, and Oscar came to him.

"It's been quite a day." Oscar held a cup of punch. "Mrs. Gillis is in charge of the punch this year." He looked all around and lowered his voice. "Her punch is better than her piano playing."

He laughed at his father-in-law's wit, and Oscar ambled away to mingle in the crowd.

Scott stayed near the door and cast a careful eye across the partygoers. As people came and went, he noted that most people greeted him with friendliness, while some were distant or ignored him. He hoped people weren't moving away from their support of him and Oscar. Days like today could boost a person's confidence in their public leaders or cause them to shift in other directions.

The rally next week would be the best opportunity to share their goals with the people of Gran Colina.

Lord, it's in Your hands.

One song ended, and another began. The swirl of a dark brown skirt caught his eye across the room. Rena danced with her father. She smiled as he talked to her. It was a welcome sign after the events of the day.

He was surprised to see Gilbert Jefferson enter the barn with Libbie Henderson on his arm. The two had never been seen together as far as he knew.

Russell Henderson and his wife followed Gilbert and their daughter into the barn.

Gilbert stopped in front of Scott. "Where's your wife, Sheriff? Can't say I've seen you too far from her since you got married."

Scott greeted the Hendersons and their daughter. "How are you folks tonight? I hope you enjoy the dance."

"Thank you, Sheriff. I'm sure we will." Mrs. Henderson excused herself and went to help at the refreshment table.

Libbie Henderson smiled at Scott, but her face resumed its neutral expression when Gilbert cut his eyes at her.

Gilbert pulled his arm into his side and patted Libbie's hand where it rested on his arm. "Come dance with me." The two of them walked away together, but Scott didn't know if he'd ever seen two people less suited for one another.

Charles Green joined them.

"How's your horse?" Scott had thought about the injured animal several times over the course of the afternoon.

"I think he'll heal up fine. It was a matter of principle to me."

Russell agreed. "I'm glad you brought him by today. That salve should help him to heal quicker."

Gilbert Jefferson danced by them with Libbie.

Scott was perplexed that Russell had permitted Gilbert to escort his daughter. "Russell, is Gilbert courting Libbie?"

Russell shrugged. "I think he asked her to the dance in an effort to win my vote."

"Why did you give him permission if you think that's his only motive?"

"I don't think it's his only motive, but I think he knows it could help him to be married. Especially now that you are." Scott hadn't considered that people would see his marriage as an asset to him being the sheriff.

"Besides," Russell continued, "Libbie is older than your Rena, so I can't say I'd be sorry to have her courting. These young ladies should be settled down with a babe or two by now. My Frances had three little ones by the time she was Libbie's age."

Charles pointed at his oldest daughter and young son. "There's Charlotte dancing with Michael. Sometimes I wonder if having her look after Sarah and Michael so often made her shy of courting and marriage. You're right, Russell. Our girls should be married like Rena."

Russell frowned. "I just don't know what to think about Gilbert Jefferson. I want her married, but I want the man to be of reputable character. This election seems to have brought out the worst in everyone."

Listening to these men talk about their daughters made Scott uncomfortable. He remembered Oscar's urgency when Rena had needed a husband. Was fatherhood fraught with worries like this? Was Libbie really so old that men wouldn't consider her as a wife?

Rena's baby could be a girl. If so, these worries would become Scott's worries.

I can do all things through Christ which strengtheneth me.

"Sheriff, are you okay? You look like a man carrying a wagonload of troubles." Russell pulled Scott from his thoughts.

"I'm fine." He spotted Rena at the refreshment table. "Though I do have a lot on my mind these days. What with the election and all." He lifted a hand to indicate their surroundings. "And Founder's Day is no small feat. I'm glad this one is coming to an uneventful end." He nodded at the two men. "If you'll excuse me, I think I'll dance with my wife before we head home."

He stepped up beside Rena and took one of the cups of punch. He slung his head back and swallowed the contents in one swoosh before setting the cup back on the table.

Rena turned to him. "Scott, I thought you were still off handling your sheriff duties."

"Dance with me." He took her by the arm and started to walk into the midst of the dancers, but she stood still, effectively halting his progress.

She leaned close. "I may be your wife, but every lady appreciates the courtesy of an invitation when it comes to dancing."

He stared at her. She was lovely in her new clothes. The sweetness in her eyes was as new as the garment.

He dropped his hand and removed his hat. He swept it across his middle and bowed. "Begging your pardon, ma'am. Would you do me the honor of the next dance?" He stayed in the bowed position and peeked up at her. Her pink cheeks and glowing smile were the result he'd desired.

"Stand up. People are starting to stare." She tugged on his arm.

"Not until you answer." He teetered to one side. "Be quick. I'm about to fall over."

Rena laughed and steadied him. "Yes."

"That's it? Yes?" Scott stood up straight and pressed his hat in place. "A man might be married to a woman, but he still appreciates a gracious acceptance. I've a good mind to rescind my offer."

She grabbed his arm and pulled him toward the dancers. "Oh, no you don't."

"That's more like it." He took her in his arms and winked at her.

"You are a challenge yourself, Sheriff Braden."

"I'm glad to hear it. You are much too energetic to be bored."

The blush that stained her cheeks made her lovelier than ever. He twirled her around the floor in time with the tune of the violins.

He was falling for her. Rena was thawing the frozen heart he'd buried the last time it was broken. Her warmth in spite of her circumstances refused to leave him alone. Day in and day out, little things she did grew on him. Everything, from making his favorite meals to protecting him in the face of Louise's nasty comments this afternoon, showed her consideration and worth.

Lord, have you given me the wife I needed, instead of the one I wanted?

"What are you thinking about?" Rena tugged the collar of his shirt straight and brushed it flat.

He met her gaze. "A lot of things, Rena. A whole lot of things." He spun her away from himself and pulled her back into his embrace.

Scott walked with Rena to their wagon after the next dance. It had been a long day, and he didn't want to keep her out too late. He didn't know a lot about women having babies, but he knew she was often tired. He suspected that was part of the process.

Founder's Day had held high points and low ones. The lowest point had been the argument between Rena and Thomas Freeman. A high point had been the few moments he'd managed to slip away from Rena after her father mentioned her upcoming birthday. He slid his hand into the pocket of his jacket and felt the small box hidden inside one of his gloves. The gift was extravagant, but wouldn't any new husband want to spoil his wife a little?

It might take a long time for Rena to heal after the pain Eugene Rodgers had caused her. Scott intended to do his part to help her forget.

He helped her climb up to the seat and walked around the back of the wagon in the moonlight. The night was ending on a high note for Scott. Tenuous, but high.

Scott and Rena joined in the singing of the final hymn at church the next morning. Rena had insisted that she wasn't too tired to come, but the circles under her eyes contradicted her.

Reverend Gillis read a passage of blessing from the Bible and dismissed the congregation.

Russell and Frances Henderson stopped at their bench to speak. "Sheriff, I've got a possibility for you about those cattle you want to buy."

Frances tugged on her husband's arm. "Russell, you know I don't like you to do business in the Lord's house." She smiled at Scott. "You feel free to go by the livery anytime this week. If you don't mind, I'm going to try to keep my husband from laboring on the Lord's Day."

"Yes, ma'am." Scott ushered Rena into the aisle as the Hendersons walked away.

"Would it be better to wait until after the election to buy the breeding stock?" Rena's face wore concern.

"I've got everything I need in place." He held her hand while they maneuvered the narrow church steps. She slipped her hand from his when she traversed the bottom step. It felt natural to move his hand to the small of her back as they walked across the churchyard to their wagon. "If I'm too busy with sheriff business or an election event, Russell's son, Amos, will tend the cattle for me." Scott helped Rena into their wagon.

Jack Jefferson called to him from the wagon next to them. "Not sure what you'll do about it, since you're seldom in town these days, but the accusations of that prisoner of yours are starting to cause trouble. Decent folks being questioned by you and your deputy ain't right."

In the same breath, Jefferson accused him of not doing his job and of doing it wrong. "The prisoner has a right to be judged according to the truth. If I find a witness to his claims, it could mean the difference in a guilty verdict or his justification."

"We got no cause to believe a stranger over the people of our own town. For the time being, you're the sheriff of Gran Colina. You need to fulfill your obligations."

People who'd been leaving the church now stopped to listen. Most of them stared outright while some pretended not to notice the tone of Jefferson's comments. Rena was quiet beside him. No doubt, she was remembering the aftermath of her conversation with Thomas Freeman on the day before. Scott noticed the way her hands curled around the edge of the seat.

"As sheriff, I will, no matter the person or persons involved, uphold and defend the laws of the great state of Texas." He climbed aboard the wagon and released the brake. "That is my duty to the people of Gran Colina."

"Gilbert wouldn't be accusing others with the killer sitting in jail." Jefferson refused to let the topic rest. "Of course, Gilbert wouldn't be doing anything the way you're doing it."

Rena stood up beside him. "Mr. Jefferson."

Scott said, "It's okay, Rena. Don't let him get to you."

Rena's voice was calm and measured, but didn't back down from Jack Jefferson. "There is a time and a place for your dissatisfaction to be expressed. You may do so next Saturday at the political rally and again when you place your vote in the ballot box next month. The churchyard on a Sunday is not the place."

Jefferson gave a snort of derision. "Sheriff, you need to keep your wife at home or teach her to be quiet. One would think she would have learned a lesson after the embarrassment she brought on you and herself yesterday. I'm guessing her own pa was ashamed of her then."

Ingrid Jefferson had sat quietly beside her husband throughout the conversation. The only evidence that his words might possibly be offensive to her was the slight movement of her shoulders when she sat even straighter on the wagon seat. Her eyes remained focused straight ahead.

Rena had come to Scott's defense, and he would not let her suffer for her efforts. "My wife is an intelligent woman with plenty to contribute to any conversation. Perhaps you should listen and learn something."

"I don't need a woman to tell me what to do or think. A good woman knows her place."

Scott saw Jefferson's jaw ripple as anger filled his face. At this point, Scott no longer cared if he upset the man further. "Rena is a good woman, and she makes me a better person. I'm sure your wife would do the same for you if you paid her any heed." Scott lifted the reins and urged the team of horses to begin their journey home.

Rena was silent until they were clear of town. "I'm so sorry, Scott. You are right. I shouldn't have let him get to me." She hung her head. "I hate to admit it, but Mr. Jefferson was right, too. I should've been quiet."

"I only wanted to protect you from his sharp tongue. I had no desire to silence you." He took her hand in his. "He was not right in his thinking about a woman's place."

"And I never intended for my words to draw your character or authority into question."

"It's becoming more and more apparent that Thomas Freeman and Jack Jefferson are working with Gilbert to cast aspersions on me. I hope your father is able to escape their efforts." He grimaced at his next thought. "They seem to have chosen you as their way to get to me."

Scott had been faithful to his duties as the sheriff of Gran Colina. Why would God allow this election to put his reputation at risk? He'd come to believe that his job as sheriff was to fight for what was right. He knew that being good wasn't enough to win against deliberate evil attacks. He also knew he couldn't win without God's help. Neither would Oscar.

On Thursday, Rena rode into town with Scott. Her clothes were ready for her at Opal Pennington's shop. A brisk wind promised an unusually cool day.

"What will you do with the rest of your day?" Scott helped her from the wagon.

"I thought I'd visit with my father and check in on Charlotte. She's been a bit out of sorts since Founder's Day. It seems her parents refused a potential suitor without speaking to her about it."

"I'm sure they have her best interest at heart."

Rena drew her cape closer around her middle. "She knows that, but seeing Libbie courting made her sad."

"Sad? I'd think any woman would be sad for the

woman who was being courted by Gilbert Jefferson."
Scott's blustered response made her laugh.

"Not everyone sees him as their enemy. He's a relatively young man of reasonable means. Once a girl passes a certain age, that's often the best she can hope for."

Scott shook his head. "Well, I hope you're able to persuade Charlotte to wait for a man who has more character than money. Money can vanish, but a man of faith and wisdom will be blessed by God to care for his family."

His impassioned words rang true. "You have proved that to me."

"I wasn't talking about myself." He pulled at the collar of his jacket. "Charlotte is a fine young lady. Charles and Nancy are good parents to her. I don't want her to fall into problems because she doesn't listen to them. She could ruin her life."

Rena felt the blood leave her face. She pulled her lips in and bit down on them to prevent the hurt that echoed through her heart at his words from bursting forth in words she would later regret. He immediately tried to retract his words.

"Rena, I didn't mean—"

"I know." It took all of her effort to get the words out. "Don't apologize. We both know the truth."

"But I am sorry, Rena."

"I'm going to see Opal now."

"Okay. I'll meet you at the hotel for lunch. About noon?"

"That will be fine."

Opal came out of the back room when Rena entered her shop. "Ah, you made it. I think you're going to be very happy."

Rena spent the next half hour trying on the different outfits that Opal had made for her.

"I think this one may be my favorite." Rena looked at her reflection in the large mirrors. The blue dress wasn't too full, nor was it fitted close to her growing form. The soft lines were exactly what she needed in her new clothes. The way this dress was made would enable her to wear it through much of her pregnancy and give her years of use beyond the time of the child's birth.

"The color is perfect for your complexion, and the pattern made up so nicely with this fabric." Opal knelt at Rena's feet to check the hemline. "Perfect." She stood and made a motion with her hand for Rena to turn and show her the opposite side. "You are lovely. Lovelier than usual."

"You're very kind. Thank you."

Opal lifted a hand to rest against her face and tapped a finger against her temple. "But something isn't right." Her scrutiny became pointed. "The something that is wrong is on the inside."

"I'm fine." Rena stepped off the platform, but Opal didn't move. "Really. I'm fine."

"Do you remember my Ophelia?" Opal's eyes misted over. "A fever took her from me when she was fourteen. My husband died that same week."

"I do remember her. She was very sweet. I was fourteen when my mother passed."

Opal seemed lost in faraway thoughts. "Sometimes when I'm making a dress, I think about how pretty Ophelia would be now. I think that is when I do some of my best work." She reached out to straighten the folds of the skirt Rena wore. "When I make your clothes, I often think of her."

"I'm honored that I bring to mind thoughts of someone so precious."

"It seems to me that you and I need one another. I don't think it's just my imagination that you could use a mother's advice. You're facing a lot of things for the first time."

Rena couldn't voice the things that she knew that Opal had discerned. She reached out and hugged her. "I do miss Momma."

"You may not be ready to talk about anything, but when you are, I'm here for you."

"That means the world to me. Please keep me in your prayers."

"I will." Opal dabbed at her eyes with a handkerchief and tucked it back into the waistband of her skirt. "Now, on to the matters at hand. Three ladies asked me to make new dresses for them after they saw you at the Founder's Day festivities."

"That's wonderful news. I think I'll wear this on Saturday." She twisted to see her reflection from another angle.

"You want to look your best at the political rally. I do hope your father and husband are successful in the elections. If you ask me, too much is said about folks when there's an election to be won." She gathered all the clothes that Rena had tried on. "I'll get these boxed up, while you get yourself back together." She nodded her head at Rena. "I can take care of that one after you've changed to the dress you wore in today."

As Rena left the shop, she thanked Opal for all of her work. "And thank you for your support of Papa and Scott. It means a lot to me."

"I wish I could vote myself. I'd gladly do it."

"Maybe one day we'll both be able to vote. This year, I'll settle for a peaceful election and our town remaining secure."

Rena took her things to Scott's office. He wasn't there, so she left the door open and stacked the two dress boxes in a corner.

"Hello, Mrs. Braden." Vernon Ramsey's voice wasn't as strong as the last time she'd been by the office and seen him.

"Are you unwell, Mr. Ramsey?" She stayed by Scott's desk, careful to be in full sight of anyone who might pass by the open doorway.

"Can't say that I am. My trial is less than a month away, and your husband has found no witness." He hung his hands through the bars and leaned his head against the front of the cell.

"I'm truly sorry. As I'm sorry for the family of the man who died."

"Gordon didn't have family. Only me."

"You were family?"

"No. I was the only friend he had in the world though. He was a disagreeable sort. We'd been friends for a couple of years. Worked odd jobs now and again as we made our way toward California. He said he wanted to see the ocean."

Rena remembered the postcard from Eugene and the newspaper article that implied the man and his dreams had died at sea. "Sadly, Mr. Ramsey, not all dreams bring happiness."

"Just the same, a man needs hope. I'm in here, and I'm losing mine."

"It's another month. You should pray. If you're telling the truth, God could let it be known." She looked through the door and back at him. "Have you spoken to the preacher?"

"No preacher wants to talk to me, ma'am."

"Reverend Gillis is a good man. If you'd like, I can ask him to come by for a visit."

Steps behind her drew Rena's attention.

"Rena, why are you here?" Scott stood in the doorway.

"I brought by the parcels from Opal's shop." She pointed at the boxes.

"You shouldn't be here alone with a prisoner." He held the door wide and motioned for her to step outside.

"The door is open, and I've stayed on this side of your desk. I was offering to ask Reverend Gillis to come see him."

Scott softened a bit, but he still waited for her to exit. "Mr. Ramsey, you'll excuse us." Rena said goodbye to the man and went through the door. Scott stayed in the doorway, but turned his back on Vernon Ramsey.

Rena knew her displeasure showed on her face. "I was not doing anything wrong, Scott."

"I know, but we've got to avoid any hint of impropriety."

Gilbert Jefferson sauntered across the street. "I see you're at work today, but you've brought your wife with you." He snickered and propped one boot on the bottom step of the porch. "Can't bear to be apart?"

Scott held up a hand. "Don't be rude, Gilbert. I'm in no mood to tolerate foolishness."

"Sheriff!" Vernon Ramsey called from his cell.

"Not now, Ramsey, I'm busy." Scott didn't take his attention from Gilbert. "Is there anything you need, Gilbert?"

"Not a thing." The arrogant attitude of the man irritated Rena to no end, but she wouldn't say anything as long as he was there.

"Sheriff! I need to speak to you." Vernon Ramsey's voice was louder this time.

"Your prisoner is calling." Gilbert laughed. "Your woman and your prisoner pulling at you from all directions. That's not how I intend to run the sheriff's office after the election."

She refused to let his arrogance go unchallenged. "You seem to have decided the will of the people before the ballots have been cast."

"The people of Gran Colina are smart enough to know when change is needed. The murder happened on your husband's watch. That makes me the right man to be sheriff. Thomas Freeman will do a much better job as mayor than your father has done." Gilbert grinned. "Don't take it personal like. Your pa's just getting old. We need someone in charge who's ready to make our town better. Not keep it the same."

"My father is a wonderful mayor. He loves this town." She took a breath. "As for the office of sheriff, I'm one of the people who was nearly killed in a bank robbery that Scott and my father thwarted."

"Those days were long ago. People forget." Gilbert tipped his hat to Rena. "Good day, Mrs. Braden. I'm sure I'll be seeing you around."

The nerve of the man. She opened her mouth but snapped it shut without a word. She would not let him goad her into further argument in the street. He walked away without another word.

Scott leaned close. "This has got to end. We can't go through the next month having our every action picked apart like we've done something wrong."

She raised her eyebrows. "You're saying we should do things in a proper manner and not worry about what is said?"

"Yes." He grunted. "And before you say anything, I know that I was just scolding you on the same principle. I'm sorry. It was unfair." He flashed that crooked smile at her. "If I do it again, you can stop me mid-sentence."

"I promise." She relaxed a bit. It was difficult, but she was determined to keep her head and not let the naysayers call her out for no reason.

The voice from inside shouted this time. "Sheriff! That was the man!"

Rena and Scott sped into the office and spoke in unison. "What man?"

"That man you were talking to was in the saloon. He was behind me. I couldn't see him, but I remember his voice."

"How do you remember it?"

"That snarl in the words and his laugh. It's downright menacing. When I heard him talking to you just now, the things he said that night came flooding back to my mind. He was harassing Gordon while we played cards. Kept laughing when Gordon would lose a hand. He finally suggested either Gordon was a terrible player or I was cheating."

Rena darted a glance at Scott. He was as engrossed in this story as she was.

Mr. Ramsey continued. "Gordon leaned over the table and told me to slide all the money to him or he'd kill me where I sat."

"How frightening." Rena wasn't accustomed to such talk. She'd walked by the outside of the saloon, but her father had forbidden her from entering. He'd told her it was no place for a woman of faith. Even during the time she refused to live her life according to God's ways, she'd never darkened the door of the place. Hearing the things that were said and done inside made her glad she'd heeded her father's wisdom.

"What happened next?" Scott had pulled a notepad from his desk and was scribbling on it.

"Gordon had been drinking." He hung his head. "We both had." Tears dropped from his chin. "I was scared. Scared to die. I knew he was my friend, but I'd seen more than one drunk man with a gun kill another fella. Then I heard Gordon pull back on the hammer of his gun. So I shot him." He wept in earnest now. The tears of remorse and guilt. "I didn't even take my gun out of the holster. If I had, he'd be sitting here, and I'd be dead." He looked up at them. "Do you think the preacher would come and pray for my soul? If they find me guilty next month, I'd like you to be able to write my ma and tell her I'd made peace with God."

Scott motioned for her to go for the preacher. She prayed for Mr. Ramsey the whole way to the parsonage. The man's plight weighed heavily on her mind. She'd been uncomfortable hearing Vernon Ramsey recount what happened that night. It frightened her to think of how people expected Scott to go into the middle of such events and restore order.

Rena knew Scott's bravery had protected her in a precarious situation.

Thinking about him in the midst of physical danger scared her in ways she couldn't fathom.

Chapter Twelve

Scott stood on the platform in front of the crowd. It looked as if every person in the county was in town for the political rally. It did his heart good to see the people engaged in the future of their community. He hoped today would show the hearts of the candidates to the people they would serve.

Oscar stepped up to the podium that someone had decorated with a red, white and blue banner. "Good afternoon, good people of Gran Colina."

Cheers reverberated through the gathering.

"We called this rally so all of you could hear from the people who have offered to serve you. We drew names from a hat to determine the order of the speakers, and I was picked to go first."

"We love you, Mayor!" Anonymous shouts rang out from those gathered. "You won't be mayor for long!"

Oscar took the rowdiness in stride. He raised both hands up. "Let me ask for your help. There are four men who will speak to you today. I'd like us to have a civil rally. All the speakers can share their thoughts. You can clap or not, cheer or not—but I'd appreciate it if there wasn't any mean-spirited conduct. We're a civil town, and after this election, we'll all have to live in the same community. We'll be glad of it in the coming months if we respect each other now."

Cheers and applause filled the air.

"Since I'm first, I'd like to affirm my promise to keep the best interest of Gran Colina in my motives and actions at all times. I pledge to you that I will not do anything that would be motivated by, or for, personal gain. I've served you these last four years with all my energy. You can count on me to continue. If you feel that I've done an earnest job for you, I'd appreciate your vote next month."

Oscar spoke for another few minutes, and Reverend Gillis called out that his time was up. Everyone laughed at Oscar's attempt to say just one more thing, only to have the preacher point him to a chair beside the other speakers.

Thomas Freeman was next. He started his speech with the smooth talk that Scott despised.

Louise Freeman stood with Rena to one side of the podium in the area set aside for the wives of the candidates. Scott saw Louise's face fill with delight when the crowd responded with laughter to a joke Thomas told. She waved at everyone when he pointed her out from the platform.

"My lovely wife is supportive of all the things I intend to do to bring Gran Colina to a higher status in the great state of Texas. It's time for us to move beyond the days of the past and become a city where people want to come and build their businesses. We'll build schools for their children and churches for their families. We'll have a town square worthy of events like the festivities that we enjoyed last week on Founder's Day and the rally we're having today."

Scott's gaze drifted to Rena. She was beautiful in her new blue dress. No one looking at her would notice the pleats at the bottom of the jacket that disguised her growing middle. Would the knowledge of the baby destroy any chance he had in the election? He hoped not.

In the last two months, he'd had plenty of time to think about his decision to marry Rena. He didn't regret it. She needed him. Her baby needed a father. Even though they didn't share the love and romantic notions of many couples who married after a lengthy courtship, they respected each other. Her friendship encouraged him. Her company made his life better.

He was beginning to think he might one day hold her in true affection. His broken heart wasn't a worthy treasure to share with Rena. It had been rendered without value by the slick words of the man speaking and the disloyal actions of Louise.

Rena smiled at him. The smile wavered in what he knew to be her nervous hope that Thomas's words would not ring true with the community. If Scott lost the election—if he caused her father to lose—one of the reasons they'd married would be gone. She could never make amends with the baby's dead father. If Scott betrayed her trust by losing the election, she could grow to despise him, too.

Lord, don't let my words or actions bring more pain to Rena.

Rena pointed at him with discreet urgency. She darted her eyes toward the podium. Laughter rang out in the crowd.

"Sheriff, it's your turn." Reverend Gillis tapped him on the shoulder.

Great. He'd drifted off in his thoughts and missed his cue. He took a deep breath and tried to gather his wits.

He stepped to the podium. "Good afternoon."

"You mean, good morning? Seems like you just woke up." The heckler evoked uproarious laughter from the gathering.

Scott was tempted to play it off as if he'd fallen into a trance because the previous speaker hadn't been able to hold his attention. He banished the thought as quickly as it came. He wasn't a man to demean another in order to lift himself. He wouldn't start today.

"My apologies for being distracted." He decided to tell the truth. "You caught me admiring my wife."

The laughter turned from acrimony to appreciation.

"It's her birthday today, and she's dressed up real nice. I was thinking about how glad I am that I asked her to marry me." He winked at Rena, and she blushed.

From that moment, the crowd was his. He silently thanked the Lord for proving, once again, that the truth will make you free. It had freed him from embarrassment and the certain ridicule of the men who would decide his future next month.

He used the biggest portion of his time to recount

the progress that had been made in crime prevention since he'd become sheriff. Some received his words, but others stood with arms crossed and hearts set against him. It was impossible to determine whether the majority supported him and Oscar or their opponents. He was convinced that his position as sheriff was tied to Oscar's without remedy. He was proud to serve with a man of such integrity.

Gilbert Jefferson followed Scott, but the interest of the people had begun to fade by the time he spoke. He spurred them out of their lethargy with one sentence.

"Do you want a sheriff who's on the job or one who's sparking with his wife and building a homestead while men are being murdered at the town saloon?"

Rena gasped. Scott wanted to rebuff Gilbert, to argue that the killing might not be a murder but a case of self-defense, to say anything to prove he hadn't been derelict in his duties. But the people would believe what they wanted to believe. Scott had done everything he could to protect the town and uphold the law. If the rantings of someone like Gilbert Jefferson could sway his supporters from that truth, so be it.

"Scott Braden isn't one of us. Why, Cyrus Busby, you've got stuff on the shelves in Busby's Mercantile that's been in Gran Colina longer than Scott Braden."

His antics were working. The crowd was swaying. Scott could see it happening before his eyes.

Gilbert took off his hat and held it over his heart. "I'm a Jefferson. The blood of the founders of our town runs through my veins. Who better to protect Gran Colina than that?" He pointed at Scott. "Of course, he's

married into the family of a founder, but that's something we didn't even see coming. For all we know, the
marriage could be for the sake of the election and not
for true affection. I'd say the women of Gran Colina
deserve true affection, and the people of Gran Colina
deserve the lifeblood of the town to course through the
leaders of the town. We don't need the spilled blood
of strangers running in our streets."

At the end of Gilbert's allotted time, cheers and
applause proved his measure of success. Scott would
pray, but he wouldn't worry. What happened next
month would have to happen. In the meantime, he
would try to find a witness to Gilbert's instigation of
the fight at the saloon.

After the rally ended, Rena stood at his elbow while
he greeted everyone who stopped to shake his hand.
The response from those who spoke to Scott and Rena
confirmed their solid backing.

When the last man walked away, he took her hand.
"Thank you for all your support."

Oscar was on the opposite side of her. "Yes, dear.
You were quite the inspiration today." He kissed her on
the temple. "I hope you're both hungry. I've asked the
Greens to put on a spread for your birthday. Nothing
off the menu tonight." He smiled. "I asked Charlotte
to help her mother choose your favorites."

"Papa, you didn't need to do that." She pulled his
hands into hers and raised up on her toes to kiss his
cheek. "But thank you."

"You two come along at your own pace. I'm going

to go ahead of you and make sure everything is perfect." Oscar left them to walk together.

Rena matched her pace to his. "Everyone loved your speech." The sun had dropped low in the sky, taking the warmth of the day with it and leaving shades of purple and orange on the horizon. She shivered and rubbed her hands over her arms.

He slid out of his jacket and draped it around her shoulders. "I don't want to spoil the look of your pretty dress. I'll take it back before we go inside the hotel."

She snuggled down into the jacket. "I may not let you." She laughed.

"You look lovely in blue."

"You don't have to say that." She stopped on the deserted sidewalk in front of Opal's store and covered her face with her hands. "And those things you said at the beginning of your speech!" She pulled her hands away a bit and peered at him over her fingers.

"I meant every word, Rena." He took her hands in his. "I was thinking about you. About how I'd marry you again tomorrow. We did the right thing."

"I'll be forever grateful." Her voice was so soft that he had to lean close to hear her.

"Would you mind if I give you your present while we're alone? Now?"

The lighthearted young lady he'd missed beamed up at him. "If you want to."

He reached into the pocket of the jacket he'd wrapped around her and pulled out the small box. "I should have given this to you earlier." He held up the gift. "I hope you like it." He tucked it into her hands.

"Scott, what have you bought?" She tugged on the ribbon that held the paper in place. She unwrapped it with care and disclosed the leather box. Her breath caught. "Oh, Scott." She lifted the lid and, in the velvet lining of the box, she found the gold ring he'd chosen.

Engraved swirls intertwined around the band in a pattern accented with golden leaves. He lifted it from the box and took her left hand in his.

"This ring symbolizes the unending promise I made to you when we got married." He slid it onto her finger. "I want you to have it as a reminder of my commitment."

She ran the thumb of her other hand across the pattern. "It's lovely." She reached up and kissed his cheek. "Thank you."

The restaurant at Green's Grand Hotel bustled with activity. Many of the people who'd attended the rally filled the tables. Charlotte showed Rena and Scott to a table near a window. Her father shared the table with Opal Pennington. Rena did her best to hide her surprise at the sight of the two of them together.

"I hope you don't mind my joining you. Your father invited me to share your table when he saw me waiting in the lobby." Opal offered a tentative smile.

"I'm delighted to have you here." Rena sat in the chair Scott held for her.

"Good evening, Mrs. Pennington." Scott sat beside Rena.

Charlotte put a hand on Rena's shoulder. "I was going to join you for supper, but we didn't realize how busy we'd be after the rally. Momma needs my help. Please forgive me."

"I'm sorry, but I understand." Rena patted Charlotte's hand.

Her friend grabbed her hand. "Oh, Rena! It's lovely!" Several people at nearby tables turned at her outburst.

Charlotte grimaced when Nancy Green shushed her. To the onlookers, she said, "I'm sorry, folks."

Rena laughed. "Thank you, Charlotte."

"What is it?" Her father craned his neck to see what all the fuss was about.

"Scott has given me a gift for my birthday." Rena held her hand so her father could see the ring.

Charlotte gave her an impromptu hug. "I have to go. Happy Birthday!" In a flourish bursting with an energy only Charlotte could manage, she was gone.

Opal took Rena's hand. "It is a lovely gift. You chose well, Sheriff. The ring and the wife."

Rena wanted to slide under the table. She was unaccustomed to such attention and flatteries.

Scott slid his arm along the back of her chair and rested his hand on her opposite shoulder. "Thank you."

Nancy Green came with a tray of plates. "The mayor has ordered a special dinner for you tonight, Rena." She set the plates on the table. "Enjoy."

"Papa, you remembered." Rena almost cried at the sight of the chicken potpies Mrs. Green had put at each place.

"Your mother would have made this for you today, if she were here." Her father cleared his throat.

Rena reached across the table and squeezed his hand. "This is perfect."

The meal was delicious, and the company was pleasant. Scott's friendly attention was a great comfort to her. The easy conversation between her father and Opal Pennington made her wonder why her father never courted anyone. Now that Rena was settled in marriage, perhaps he could consider a companion.

"This is the happiest birthday I've had since Momma—in a very long time. Thank you all."

Opal touched her napkin to the corner of her mouth. "It's been a joy for me to be a part of this special occasion."

"I feel especially pretty tonight. You did a splendid job on my new clothes."

Scott touched the sleeve of her jacket. "I haven't seen them all, but this color is a favorite."

Eli Gardner came into the restaurant. He stopped just inside the door, and his eyes searched the room. Scott stood, and Eli motioned for him.

"Oscar, will you take Rena home with you? From the look on Eli's face, I could be a while."

The lovely day and dinner were over. Scott's job intruded on their pleasant evening. She understood his duties as sheriff. Her only regret about his loyalty to the job was that some people didn't appreciate it. He was walking through the door before she had a chance to tell him goodbye. Or caution him to be careful. The danger of his work weighed on her mind with increasing trepidation in recent weeks.

"I do hope it's nothing terrible." Rena clasped her hands in her lap to keep from wringing them together.

Papa pushed his chair away from the table. "I'm sure he can handle whatever it is."

"Well, it's been a lovely supper, but it's time for me to make my way home." Opal picked up her reticule from the corner of the table.

"Will you allow us to walk with you and see you safely home?" Papa stood and pulled the back of Opal's chair as she rose.

"That won't be necessary."

"It's right on our way." Her father escorted them from the restaurant into the hotel lobby.

Several people stood around the hotel entrance looking into the street beyond.

"You ladies stay here, and I'll find out what's happening." Her father left them near the registration desk and made his way through the midst of the people at the door.

Rena followed him, and Opal pulled on her arm in an attempt to stop her. Rena shrugged her off. "Scott is out there. I can't stay in here and wonder what's happening."

"Scott needs to focus right now. If something dangerous is happening, any distraction could put him at risk."

She stopped and considered Opal's words. She remembered how he protected her during the bank robbery and almost lost his life when she distracted him. "I won't put them in danger, but I can't just stand here and wonder."

"Then you should pray for them. God can protect Scott the way he protects you."

Opal was right. Rena found a chair in a far corner. She bowed her head in silent prayer. The crowd at the doorway grew. She refused to allow it to distract her from her prayers.

The minutes crept by like hours. Opal stood a short distance from Rena and kept a watch for any sign of what was happening.

Eli Gardner yelled through the open door. "Is Doc Taylor in there?"

The echo of calls for the doctor rippled through the room and into the restaurant.

Rena bolted out of the chair. She would've gone right out the door, but Opal caught her by the hand and held her back.

Doc Taylor came from the restaurant carrying his bag. "I'm coming. I knew when they came for the sheriff I'd be next." He ambled across the lobby of the hotel in no apparent hurry. "A man can't eat a decent meal without being interrupted around here." Everyone in Gran Colina knew he didn't mean of word of his complaint. No one ever waited for his care when the need for his services arose.

Rena composure slipped away. "I have to know if it's Scott, Opal. I have to know."

"We'll all know soon."

Rena's mind raced through the memories of the last month. Scott's shock at her father's request that he marry her. The messy cabin that greeted her on her wedding day. Milking Bertie. Reading the Bible at night. Worrying when Scott returned home late. His sincere efforts to find the truth about Vernon Ramsey. The way he kissed her cheek when they got married.

She looked down at her hand and fingered the gold band. It was a gesture of friendship that promised a contented life with a man who respected her. She couldn't lose him. The fear that gripped her was paralyzing. A fear like none she'd ever known.

When Betty Alexander had shown her the news of Eugene's death, no grief had seized her. She had felt sorrow for the man but not for herself. She had not lost anything when he died.

The thought of losing Scott forced her to acknowledge her growing affection for him.

"He can't be dead. He simply can't be dead." Rena didn't realize she'd spoken aloud until Opal answered.

"Don't borrow worry. We don't know who is hurt or how badly."

Someone pushed through the crowd at the door. It was her father. He came straight to her and took her hands. "Come with me, child."

She was frozen to the spot, unable to move. "Tell me."

Chapter Thirteen

Scott's head throbbed. The darkness was heavy. Soft voices in the distance pulled at him.

He tried to lift his hand to press against the pain, but someone held it tight. The grip was firm yet gentle.

"Scott, can you hear me?" It was Rena's voice.

His throat was too dry for words, so he tried to nod. The pain in his head exploded with vehemence, and he groaned.

"He can hear you. I don't want him to try to move or talk right now." A hand pressed against his shoulder. "I'm guessing he's got a whopper of a headache." Doc Taylor's annoying voice pierced through the pain.

What had happened? The last thing he remembered was following Eli into the alley beside the saloon.

He tried to talk but couldn't.

"Will he be okay, Doc?" Rena's voice trembled in the distance.

"Probably. I need to check on Eli. I'll be back."

Scott struggled to open his eyes, but the darkness won.

When he woke again, he could see light without opening his eyes. The throbbing in his head had become a heavy ache. A tender hand still held his. Rena had not left him. With great effort, he managed to close his fingers around hers.

In an instant, she responded with a gentle squeeze. Her voice came as a whisper near his ear. "Try to stay still. Doc says you're going to be fine."

His eyes fluttered open, and he closed them tight against the glare of the light streaming through the window.

"I'll be right back." She released his hand, and he heard her soft steps as she left him.

"So you decided to wake up?" Doc Taylor's voice was harsh after Rena's quietness.

Scott squinted when he tried to open his eyes again.

"Mrs. Braden, pull that curtain across the window please."

The dimness of the room allowed him to open his eyes. Rena's drawn face was the first sight he saw. She captured his hand in hers again.

"Looks like you took the worst of it." Doc Taylor peered in his eyes and pushed his head from one side to the other.

"Ouch!" It took all his energy to say the word, and it barely sounded above a whisper.

"The headache will go away, and nothing is broken."

"Eli?" No one had told him if his deputy was badly injured.

"He's at the jail. Only took a glancing blow. A few

stitches was all he needed." The doctor looked at Rena. "Don't let him get up yet. I'll be back in a few minutes."

"You nearly scared the life out of me." She touched the side of his face with the gentleness that belied the intensity of her words.

"What happened?" He tried to swallow. "Can I have a drink of water?"

Rena nodded and poured water from a pitcher by the bed into a glass. She lifted his head just enough to help him get a drink. He struggled against the pain.

"Eli said there was a brawl at the saloon. Some of the men who had been at the rally were arguing about the election. Elmer Hicks sent someone for help." She wiped his brow with a cool cloth. "That's when Eli came for you."

"I remember that part. When we got to the saloon, the men who were fighting ran off in every direction. We were headed back to the jail when we heard the sounds of fighting in the alley by the saloon." He closed his eyes again. The pain in his head made the words difficult.

"You don't have to talk now. Just knowing that you will be okay is enough. You can sort out the details when you're stronger."

"I want you to know." He lifted his hand and brushed the creases between her eyes. "I don't want the signs of worry on your face to be on my account."

"Sometimes, Scott, the sheriff's wife worries." She smiled and sat on a chair by the bed. "I promise to pray through the worries. Close your eyes and try to rest. I'll be right here when you wake."

"I can't rest until I know what happened."

"I'll tell you all I know from Eli. The two of you followed the noise of the fight, but it was so dark that he couldn't identify the men. You told them to stop fighting or they'd have to spend the night in jail. Eli said the next thing he knew you were on the ground at his feet. Someone must have hit you from behind. The two men who were fighting ran off. When Eli tried to help you, someone hit him, too."

"That doesn't make sense. Why would someone attack us from behind?"

"Eli's been out all day looking for answers. He promised to come as soon as he knows anything."

"All day? What time is it?"

"It's after three. Doc Taylor said if you rest for a couple more hours I can take you home before supper."

He closed his eyes. "I like the sound of that." He drifted off again, grateful to know Rena would be there.

And she was there. She was there for the conversation with Eli that got them nowhere. She was there to help Eli get him into the wagon.

When they arrived at home, Amos Henderson was there doing the chores. Scott was glad he'd hired the lad to carry some of the load on the homestead for him. With Amos's help, Rena got him into the house. Doc Taylor had warned that his balance put him at risk of falling until the lump on his head went down.

He wasn't to ride a horse or climb in and out of the wagon unassisted until then.

"Are you sure you don't want to be in your bed? You can't be comfortable in that chair." Rena lit the fire that Amos had laid in the fireplace.

"It's only my head and my pride that are wounded. I'm able to sit up."

"I'll be right in to get your supper. Let me talk with Amos about what needs to be done today and get some bacon from the smokehouse."

He stood up slowly. "I can have a word with Amos and get the bacon. You've done enough."

"Would you please give me the peace of mind of knowing that you'll rest today? If you wake up tomorrow feeling better, I won't object to you working at whatever you choose to do."

He eased back into the chair. "Just today."

She smiled. "I'll be quick."

By the time they finished their supper, he was much more himself. They sat in front of the fire, and Rena read a chapter from the Bible.

"Your voice is restful. Much easier on a man with a monstrous headache than the barked orders of a doctor who has no sympathy for your plight." He tried to join in with her laughter, but the pain in his head forbade it.

She put aside her Bible and pulled her chair closer to the hearth. She propped her feet up on its edge, and he noticed her swollen ankles.

"Do your feet hurt?"

"No." She tugged her skirt to cover her ankles.

"Doc Taylor says the swelling is common for someone in my condition."

Scott leaned forward. "I didn't know the doctor was aware of your condition."

"He wasn't. He noticed my feet last night and asked if I was with child." She stared into the fire. "He told me he already suspected. It seems the town doctor is very observant."

"I guess it won't be long before almost everyone knows."

"It's not a secret that can be hidden for long." Rena put her hand on her growing midsection. "He said something else that was meant to be a comfort but was troubling, nonetheless."

"What?" Scott didn't like the worry in her voice.

"He warned me not to be upset if people thought it was too soon for us to have a child. He said he's delivered babies born very early and even a few who came late. That they come in all different sizes, too, so not to mind if anyone made comments if the baby arrived early." She studied the floor at her feet. "He said people love a good gossip, but they move on as soon as the next thing comes along."

Scott didn't like the thought of Rena being the object of gossip, but it had been a very real possibility from the beginning. "I agree with the doctor. We can't help what folks might say." He got up and added a log to the fireplace. "Why don't we turn in? It's been a long couple of days for both of us."

"You're right." She headed for her bedroom. "Do you need anything before you lie down?"

"Just to apologize for ruining your birthday dinner."

"The dinner was wonderful." She held up her hand and looked down at her ring. "Thank you for the lovely gift. It was very generous."

"I'm glad you're pleased." An awkward silence hung between them.

"Well, good night then." She took a step away from him. "I'll thank the Lord for answering my prayers for your safety when I pray tonight." Her eyes were misty when she said, "I don't know what I would do if something happened to you."

She went into her room and closed the door.

Hearing Rena say that she prayed for him sank into the fissures of his wounded soul with more healing power than anything the doctor had done to tend his physical injuries.

Rena watched through the front window as she washed the dishes on Thursday after lunch. Scott could return at any time. He had stayed home until midday on Monday but had worked in town every day since. He'd insisted that it was unfair to leave all the work to Eli. The swelling of the lump on his head had decreased with each passing day, and the doctor said he would have no lasting effects from the injury.

The only clue as to who might have ambushed the two of them came from Vernon Ramsey. He claimed to have overheard some men talking about making the sheriff look foolish. Their voices had come from behind the jail, but Vernon had been unable to see them. Once again, the fact that he was from out of town hindered any investigation Scott or Eli tried to conduct with information they received from him.

She dried the last plate and put it on the shelf. A shrill whistle in the distance caught her attention, and she went out on the front porch. Scott and Amos drove the small starter herd down the lane.

Rena smiled and waved a dish towel over her head. Scott responded by waving his hat in the air. He had worked for this day for a long time. His homestead was becoming a ranch. Ten cows and a bull were the first step in fulfilling his dream. After all his sacrifices for herself and others, Rena was happy to see something he wanted come to be.

It only took a few minutes for Scott and Amos to drive the cattle through the gate and into the corral.

"Amos, let's get them watered." Scott pulled the wide gate closed.

Rena hung over the corral fence and watched the cows test the boundaries of their new home. "Oh, Scott, they look fine."

"Russell Henderson assured me that they come from the finest stock he could locate."

"Life will surely be different around here now." Rena laughed as the bull snorted and shook his head near the new gate.

"I'm glad to see this day come." Scott slid out of the saddle and tied Copper to the corral fence.

Rena flung the dish towel over one shoulder and backed away from the fence. "Come to the cabin when you finish. I have pie waiting for both of you."

Amos left for home as soon as he finished his pie,

and Scott went back to the barn to do the evening chores. Rena stirred the stew that simmered on the stove. It wouldn't be ready for another hour. She sat at the table again and continued to piece together the small quilt she was making for her child. The top was almost complete by the time Scott entered the cabin.

He hung his hat on the peg by the door. "I'm real pleased. The animals are healthy, and the fence is sound. I'm feeling so good about things that I'm considering naming the ranch." He stoked the fire and sat on the hearth.

"I think that's fitting. Do you have a name in mind?" Rena stood and picked up the quilt top. It was time to set the table.

"I'll have to think on it for a bit." Scott came to stand on the opposite side of the table and pointed at her handiwork. "Can I see that?"

Rena laid the quilt top out so he could inspect the pattern. "It's my first attempt."

Scott ran his hand across the starburst pattern. "It's like the one my mother made for me."

"I hope you don't mind. I used it as a guide."

"Why would I mind? I treasure that quilt because of the love and effort my mother put into every stitch." His thoughtful gaze brought her a moment of joy. "I'm sure your child will treasure this." The moment ended. *Your child.* She longed for him to consider the child to be his own but knew it was unfair to hope or ask for such a thing.

She picked up the quilt top and folded it. "I hope so." She tucked the workings of the quilt into her sewing basket and set it aside. "I'll have supper on the table in a minute."

While she dished up the stew, he pulled the cradle out of the corner by the fireplace. "I hope I can finish sanding this tonight."

"You had a busy week. Are you sure you don't want to rest?"

"I couldn't sleep. I'm wound tighter than an eight-day clock. Finally having the cattle and dealing with my responsibilities as sheriff has my mind busy. Sanding on this cradle may help clear my head."

Rena put the butter on the table beside the bread and poured them both a cup of coffee. "It's ready." She took a seat and waited for him to join her.

"It smells delicious. Just that short distance to get the cattle from the train station to here gave me quite an appetite." He offered a blessing over the food and picked up a slice of bread.

"What kind of sheriff duties kept you busy today?"

"Eli thinks he knows who ambushed us. There's a couple of new hands out at Jefferson's ranch. Eli saw them talking to Gilbert outside of the saloon last night."

"Did you arrest them?"

"No. It's only a hunch." He dipped his bread in the gravy. "I think Eli is onto something, but I don't think there's any way to prove it."

"If only Vernon Ramsey had seen them."

"Those windows are small and positioned high on the cell walls to keep the prisoners from reaching them. This is one time when it didn't work in our favor." He shrugged. "Truth be told, we don't really know if we can take Vernon at his word. I still haven't found anyone to back up his story."

"I'll keep praying." These days it seemed like praying was all she did. It frightened her to know there were people who wanted Scott out of office so badly that they'd ambush him in the night.

"To make things worse, Gilbert Jefferson is insinuating that being attacked proved that I shouldn't be the sheriff."

"Surely people won't have forgotten how awful things were when Gilbert Jefferson was sheriff." Her father had decided to run for the office of mayor the first time because of Gilbert Jefferson's deliberate refusal to deal with the crime that had frightened people off the streets at night. "The last two years are the most peaceful this town has known. Until Vernon Ramsey and Gordon Dixon came to town."

He dropped his spoon into his empty bowl. "It's getting out of hand, Rena. I could lose the election."

The next day, Scott headed to the mercantile for supplies for his office but stopped just short of the corner. Betty Alexander's voice, clear and crisp, reached his ears. "Rena Braden was the only person Eugene Rodgers communicated with after he left Gran Colina. I think that baby belongs to him. You'll never be able to convince me different." Scott glanced around the corner and saw her back as she stood on the sidewalk in front of the store. Rena had been right when she'd said people would start to notice her pregnancy.

"Betty, you shouldn't say such things. Rena is married to the sheriff. It's scandalous to spread such rumors." Opal Pennington's words were quiet.

"It's not scandalous if it's true. She only married the sheriff after that fellow left town. And now, so soon, she's expecting a child. It's not right, I tell you. It's just not right."

Scott could listen no longer. He stepped around the corner and stood in front of Betty Alexander. Shock at seeing him covered her face.

"Sheriff, I didn't see you come up."

"Really? I'm surprised you didn't notice me standing right there." He pointed to the corner of the building. "I plainly heard your conversation. I must caution you, Miss Alexander, about repeating such matters as you've just been discussing."

He touched the brim of his hat. "Mrs. Pennington." He greeted Rena's friend with a smile that disappeared when he returned his attention to Betty. "Mrs. Pennington has given you wise counsel. You wouldn't want anyone to accuse you of slandering a fellow citizen of our community. To do so could injure the other person and cause people to think poorly of you for carrying the tale."

She gave a smug tilt of her head. "I will not be threatened into silence by you, Sheriff. The truth is the truth. The matter bears importance as you are running in this election. The people of Gran Colina have a right to know the true character of the candidates and their families."

"Ah, the true character of a person. That is a good

thing to know." He took in a slow breath. "Then let me speak to that, and that alone. My wife is a woman of great character. You will not find a woman more committed to God or her family. She would do anything for them. I promise you won't find her whispering in the shadows about things she suspects or imagines. Our marriage took place in the church and before our friends and family. The courtesy of your respect for our union would be the proper response."

She opened her mouth, but he held up a hand and continued.

"You told me yourself that you read the only postcard Rena received from Eugene Rodgers. There was no indication whatsoever on that card of any relationship between them. I am certain, given your concerted attention to detail about anything that goes through the post office, that had my wife corresponded with Eugene Rodgers—or any other man—you would be aware of it."

Opal put a hand on Betty's arm. "Matters, such as this, are best left alone. I see no reason to think the rumors are true. No one is bettered for discussing them."

Betty narrowed her eyes on Scott. "Consider yourself warned, Sheriff. I am not the only one who doesn't believe the two of you married without cause. You may have stood in the shadows and overheard my words, but I'm not the only one talking." She turned on her heel and went away in a huff.

Opal tried to console him. "Don't worry. Good people don't listen to gossip."

"There's the problem, Mrs. Pennington. Voting is a right for every man. Not just the good ones."

He watched Betty Alexander enter the post office and close the door with a decided thump. No doubt, she would add his response to her gossip the next time she shared her opinion. He had every expectation that she would continue to spread it—to anyone who would listen.

After service the following Sunday, Scott sat with Rena in the empty church. The sunlight of the spring day flooded through the windows and bathed the room around them in warmth.

She'd brought her mother's Bible with her to ask the preacher some questions about notes her mother had made on the pages. He'd done his best to help her understand the personal thoughts and left them.

"I miss her." Rena stared at the front of the church. "We sat on this very bench every Sunday. She had the most beautiful singing voice." She smiled at the memory. "She and Papa were happy. Happier than any married couple I've ever known."

Scott didn't know what to say, so he listened.

"I need her now. There are so many things happening to me that she would be able to help me with. She could teach me to care for the baby. I'm scared, Scott, and I don't know what to do. I keep thinking that if she hadn't died, I would never have stopped coming to church. I would never have been tempted by the likes of Eugene Rodgers." She looked at him. "But even that isn't fair. I can't blame him alone. I was a party to my own wrongdoing."

He held out a hand. "May I hold the Bible?"

She passed it to him, and he flipped through the pages. "I want to show you a passage that helps me when I'm bogged down in the past." He found the verses he wanted to share with her in Philippians and read it aloud. "Brethren, I count not myself to have apprehended: but this one thing I do, forgetting those things which are behind, and reaching forth unto those things which are before, I press toward the mark for the prize of the high calling of God in Christ Jesus."

He handed the Bible back to her. "I know you have a lot of respect for your mother, and you've learned a lot from her notes in here. Don't you think it's time you started making your own notes?"

She turned to him. "But I don't know what to write. I can learn from her, but I don't have anything to teach others." She held a hand to her midsection. "I'll share my mother's lessons with my baby, but how can I teach my child things that I haven't done myself."

"That's what it means, Rena. You can forget the past. All of it. The pain. Wrong choices. You can forget that and look to your future. Your child is your future. The notes you make in here—" he pointed at the Bible "—will mingle with your mother's. Your child will learn about God and faith from you and from her."

"Thank you." She grasped his hand. "Again. I think I've learned as much from you as I have from my parents."

"We both have a lot to learn. About life and faith."

He stood and pulled her to her feet. "We can learn it together. I think the first thing we need to do is forget the past."

She nodded. "I'll try."

"Sometimes the things of faith have to be done over and over again until they stick. We can forget a little more every day, because His mercies are new every morning." He walked with her to the door. "Concentrating on our future will make it easier."

They stepped into the bright sunshine. "The future is going to be here before we know it. The herd will grow. The election is just over two weeks away. Then the trial."

He raised his eyebrows. "And then the baby."

Scott led her to the wagon with the distinct impression that they'd both have to remember to forget a lot of things in life. Given what he was learning about the people of Gran Colina during this election, he decided most people had things that would be best forgotten.

He hoped they'd remember the good things. He hoped someone would remember whether or not there'd been a gun in the hand of the man Vernon Ramsey had shot.

He hoped Rena could forget the time she'd spent away from her faith.

And he hoped he could forget the pain of the broken heart that had begun to heal.

They ate lunch with her father and Opal Pennington. Oscar had invited Opal to join them.

"Papa, when you invited us to lunch, I thought we'd

be treated to something you had Mrs. Green cook for you."

"I hope that means you enjoyed your lunch." Her father stood by the fireplace in the parlor.

"I did." She smiled at him. "Though I suspect Opal had a hand in the meal."

"I did offer some help with the stew, but your father was the one who cooked it." Opal sat on the settee with Rena. "After I put it all in the pot for him."

Everyone laughed.

Rena turned to him, and he caught the merry twinkle in her eye. She was happy here. Her relationship with her father had stood the test that would have divided many families forever. It was a comfort to see the healing power of forgiveness at work.

"Oscar, since you're taking lessons in cooking, do you think you might want to bring me lunch at the sheriff's office sometimes?"

"Scott, you know a man will put up with a woman telling him what to put in a pot of stew a whole lot quicker than he'll tolerate another man teasing him about it." Oscar grinned. "No. I won't bring you lunch. You came in here and stole away my last cook." He started to chuckle, but it caught in his throat.

Scott shot a quick glance at Rena. She fidgeted in the chair she'd always sat in when he used to come to supper before they'd married. Had that really been over two months ago?

"I am a blessed man to have the finest cook in Gran Colina." Scott didn't look away from Rena as he did his best to cover Oscar's awkward statement.

The relief in Rena's face was worth the effort.

"Papa, tell me how you convinced Opal to join us for a meal."

Oscar focused on Opal's face. "It seems that Opal and I have quite a lot in common. We have things that complement each other."

"Pray tell, what sort of things, Papa?"

"Well, first of all, she likes to cook, and I like to eat." Oscar counted off the reasons on his fingers. "Second, she's pretty, and I enjoy beauty."

Opal blushed like a young bride at his open praise of her. "You're embarrassing me, Oscar."

"Feel free to share the things you like about me, if that will make you feel better," Oscar teased her mercilessly.

"Okay, I sing soprano, and your father sings bass. Harmony is a good thing."

"Oh, I have another." Oscar counted off another finger. "I don't enjoy the thought of getting old, and Opal makes me feel young again."

Rena had been silent while her father and Opal had gone on about each other.

"If it disturbs you for me to be here, I understand, Rena." Opal was an honest person. Sometimes too honest and forthright.

Scott was concerned that her silence would be interpreted as disapproval.

Oscar came to stand by Opal and rested a hand on her shoulder. "Please tell us if we've upset you."

"Not in the least." She went to wrap her father in a hug. "My only hope is for you to be happy." She hugged Opal. "This dear lady has been a blessing in my life. I think she's a lovely addition to yours."

Oscar and Opal were both relieved at Rena's kind acceptance.

"In that case, Opal, I'd like to ask your permission to come calling." Oscar tugged on the bottom of the vest he wore. "Be aware that I intend to call often and with great seriousness."

Opal put a hand on his arm. They stood by the fireplace and stared into each other's faces. The picture they made was as good as any portrait Scott had ever seen.

"You have my permission. But you must not be so serious as to lose the fun of who you are."

Scott and Rena left soon after the acceptance of a formal courtship.

Oscar seemed to be happier when Opal was around. Rena moving out of his home must have left a great void.

As Scott held Rena's hand and she climbed into the wagon, he thought of how she'd filled the emptiness at his home. The homestead was a new place since she'd come to live there. Then it came to him.

"Rena." His eyes grew wide. "I've come up with a name for the ranch."

"What?" Her eyes shone with anticipation. He loved that she'd embraced the things that mattered to him.

"New Dawn Ranch." He settled into the seat beside her and released the brake. "It's become a place of new beginnings. My dreams of being a rancher are happening."

"My new life started there." She touched her tummy. "The baby will be a new life there." Her face lit up with joy. "I love it. New Dawn Ranch."

They were riding through the middle of town on their way home when Eli stepped off the porch of the jail. Scott pulled the wagon to a stop.

"Afternoon, Eli."

"Sheriff. Mrs. Braden." Eli tipped his hat to her. "Sheriff, can I talk to you?"

Rena moved to the edge of her seat and asked Eli to assist her. "I think I'll drop in on Opal while you two talk. She mentioned that she was going home as we left and had something she wanted to show me when I had time."

Scott climbed from the wagon. "I'll come for you when I finish here."

"There's no rush." Rena waved and headed back the way they'd come.

"Sheriff, I went to the mercantile yesterday for supplies." Eli lowered his voice. "I don't want your missus to hear, but there was talk." He cut his eyes over his shoulder. "Cyrus has decided that you and Mrs. Braden were, um, were, I don't know how to say it."

Scott didn't like the sound of this. "Just say what you heard, Eli."

"He said folks are saying your missus is, um, in the family way."

"She's a married woman, Eli. Children are a blessing."

"But that's not how he said it." Eli looked up and

down the street. "He's saying you haven't been married for long. He's hinting at things a man ought not to say."

He'd known this was a possibility, but he hadn't expected so many attacks from so many directions. "He's a busy man, Eli. Busy talking about other folks. Everyone who knows Cyrus knows that." He walked past him toward the door. "Don't let him worry you. There's nothing bad to be said about a married couple having a child."

Eli didn't agree. "You can brush it off like a fly on a cake if you want to, Sheriff, but this pest ain't gonna leave you alone. Too many people are buzzing with the notion of it."

Scott was beginning to think Eli might be right.

Opal welcomed Rena and offered to make a pot of tea. "I'm glad you've come, but a bit surprised to see you so soon."

"Scott and I were on our way home when Eli Gardner wanted to speak to Scott." Rena sat on the settee in Opal's parlor. "We hadn't been married long before I discovered that Scott's position as sheriff is unending. There are countless times when he's called on in the night or works until the early morning hours."

"It seems the more Gran Colina grows, the more we need the sheriff." Opal brought the tea things on a tray and set it on the table in front of the settee. "I'm not certain how things will go if he doesn't win the election."

"Thank you." Rena accepted the offered teacup. "I hate to think how my father will react if the two of them don't win the election. They've both worked so hard to improve the safety of our town. Some towns are filled with notorious criminals or ruled by fear and lawless gangs. We are blessed to enjoy the safety and peace we have."

"Living alone as I do—and across the street from Mabel's Saloon—I'm appreciative of the way the sheriff and your father enforce the laws." Opal added sugar to her tea and stirred it.

"It's only a couple of weeks until the election. I hope things will settle down after that. I don't enjoy the snide remarks or petty comments I've heard."

Opal set her cup down. "So the sheriff told you about the things Betty said? I'm glad."

"What things?"

"I'm sorry. I thought that's what you were referring to. I wouldn't have brought it up if I'd known he hadn't told you."

Rena knew it must be unpleasant business if Scott hadn't mentioned it to her. "Please tell me. I want to be able to help Scott any way I can. I can't do that if I don't know what he's being confronted with."

"I don't want to tell you. It could hurt you, but I'd rather you hear it from me than to be surprised by it on the street."

"It must be dreadful."

"I tried to convince her not to say such things."

"Please just say it outright. I can't think it will be easier to bear by the slow telling of it." She didn't want to be curt with her friend, but she hoped what Betty Alexander had said wouldn't be as difficult to bear as the wondering. "I'm imagining all sorts of horrid things."

Opal took a deep breath. "She's stirring the idea that your child could belong to the man who left town a few weeks before your marriage. Eugene Rodgers." She took Rena's hand. "I'm so sorry to say such a thing to you. It seems Betty is determined to repeat this tale, and she even said others were speculating about your marriage and the child."

Rena dropped her gaze to her lap. She deserved to be the object of scorn, but Scott didn't. How could she fight against the truth? Even if she did, they had no guarantee it wouldn't be believed.

Opal apologized. "If there had been a way for you to never know what she's said, I'd have chosen it. Gossip is an ugly thing. It grows and festers. The telling of it intrigues the teller and can bring irreparable harm to the subject. I tried to stop her from repeating the words. So did the sheriff, but she was determined."

Rena trembled inside. She and Scott had just talked about moving forward, but her sin was ever before her. "Thank you for your honesty. I'm not certain there is a way to combat this."

"Rena, you can't let what people say rule your life. You have a fine, Christian husband. I've seen the changes you've made in the last few months. It's done my heart a world of good to see you sitting in the church by your pa." She shook her head. "Those years you weren't there wore heavy on his heart."

"I would give anything to do those years over."

"We all have that feeling about some part of our

life." She patted Rena's hand. "You are in my prayers, child."

Opal treated her like she imagined her mother would have treated her. With honesty and kindness.

Rena picked up the tray. "Let me help you wash up."

"First, I have something I want you to see."

She put the tray down and followed Opal out of the living quarters and into the shop.

Opal lifted a basket from the back corner of the room. "I thought you might like these." She offered the basket to Rena.

The basket was filled with tiny clothes. Every imaginable shade of green, blue and yellow had been made into gowns and shirts for a little one.

"Oh, these are beautiful." Rena lifted out the delicate items and admired them.

"I hope you don't think me intrusive." Opal stood with her hands clasped in front of her.

"I think this is the kindest thing anyone could have done for me at this season of my life." She pulled her friend into a hug. "Thank you."

"I'm sure that if your mother was here, this is the sort of thing she'd have done. I know that's what I'd have done for my Ophelia."

"I've been missing her more than usual this last few months." Rena sniffed against the threatening tears. "I'm honored to receive a gift made with so much love."

"I kept thinking of a little girl. Even if the child is a boy, these patterns will work." She smiled. "I could teach you to sew if you like."

"That would be wonderful."

A knock at the door announced Scott's arrival. Rena carried the basket in her hands and the love of her new dear friend in her heart.

God, help me to treasure the gift of this friendship. Thank You for sending Opal to fill the painful hole of my mother's absence. Help me to be a comfort to her as she continues to live without her precious daughter.

Scott arched his back to stretch out his aching muscles and wiped his brow with the sleeve of his shirt. The last week of March was warm, but not as warm as it would be in a couple of weeks.

Rena stepped out on the back porch. "I've made you some lunch. You could come in out of the sun for a few minutes."

"That sounds good." He followed her into the house.

She offered him a plate of cold ham and potato salad. "How much longer do you think you'll be working on the garden?"

"I should be able to get the seed in the ground this afternoon."

"Let me help with that." She sat across from him at the table. The windows were open and a breeze blew through the room.

"I think I can manage."

Rena cut a slice of bread and handed it to him. "Our agreement was for me to help."

He tore the bread in half. "Do you know anything about a garden?"

"Not much, but you can teach me."

"I'll show you what to do, but we'll have to work quickly. We've had so much rain this season that it'll be good for the crop, but the seed needs to be covered up so it won't wash away if we get more rain tonight."

"Let's pray it won't rain. I'm looking forward to the fresh vegetables."

Scott agreed. "Some green beans would make this meal perfect."

"I'd love carrots. Lots of carrots." They finished their meal before heading into the garden.

He showed her how to drop the seed into the rows, and he came behind her and covered them. She had never planted a garden before, and it showed.

"Wait." He scooped out the extra seeds she'd dropped into one spot. "We'll run out of seed at the rate you're going. And the plants will be so close together that the yield will be choked out."

"I'm sorry." She handed him the seed packet. "Show me again."

By the third row, they were working together well. "I love corn, but are you sure we need this much?" She worked down the row from him.

"We'll need some for the extra hogs."

"We're going to have more hogs?"

He laughed. "Yes. That's where the bacon and ham come from, silly girl."

Rena turned on him. "I know where pork comes from. I'm a girl from town, but I'm not uneducated."

"Well—" he pointed "—how do you explain that?"

She looked down at her feet and saw the contents

of two seed packets puddled in the dirt. She shrugged. "Maybe I'm not as well versed as I need to be."

He gathered as much of the spilled seed as he could. "Since you like carrots so much, you should guard the carrot seeds better." He moved over to the rows they'd designated for carrots and started to plant them.

"They must have slipped out of my apron when I stooped over to plant the corn."

"The first time I helped my mother with a garden, I pulled up all the bean plants because I thought they were weeds. She came out to find me happy with my work, only to discover my mistake."

"What did she do?"

"If I remember right, she said something about, 'Scott, what am I going to do with you?' and then tousled my hair."

"Did you have beans that year?"

"Yes. It was early spring, so she was able to get more seed. After that, I wasn't allowed to weed the garden unless she was with me."

"She didn't scold you?"

"Nope. She taught me. She knew I was trying to help."

"That's a sweet memory."

"Most of my memories of my mother are of her teaching me something."

They finished the last row and gathered their tools.

"I would love to have known her." Rena followed him to the barn and helped put away the tools.

"She was a good woman. Quiet and settled. I never met anyone more determined or strong. After our pa died, she worked odd jobs to put food on the table for Ann and me."

"You must miss her." Rena was quiet. Reflective.

"I do. Probably the same way you miss your mother."

She sat on a bench. "Momma meant the world to me. We did everything together. When she died, it was like part of me died with her."

"I'm sorry for your loss."

"Everyone says that. They're sorry." She stared into the distance. "I'm sorry, too. Sorry for the things I didn't learn from her. Sorry that she'll never know her grandchild. Sorry for all the things that should have been and weren't." She threw her head back and clinched her fists. "Life got so much harder after she died."

He didn't know what to say. Her pain was vivid.

She looked at him. "I'm sorry that she didn't get to meet you. She'd have loved you for the way you helped me and the baby. And Papa."

"Tell me about her."

For the next hour, Rena shared stories of her childhood. The laughter and love in the Livingston home was strong. Their faith was a mainstay. He wondered that she'd ever abandoned hers.

Seeing into her world—the past that had shaped her and still held her in its grasp—helped him understand her. The things he'd dismissed as flightiness before they'd married were attempts to bring back the essence of the fun she'd known as a child.

"Your mother sounds like a wonderful person. I'm glad you have the lessons she left you in her Bible.

She must have been a great teacher." He stood and moved to Copper's stall to begin his evening chores. "Even if she didn't teach you how to plant a garden." He winked at her gasp. "I'm glad she taught you to cook. Would you mind using that skill while I handle the chores out here?"

"Oh, I don't know. Maybe I should make you cook supper and see if you need some lessons from me." She laughed and left him to his work.

Somehow, delving into the part of her heart where she'd buried the treasure that was her mother's memory cast Rena in a new light. There was a joyous person inside her who would be a great mother. He prayed she would find that person and share her with the child she carried.

Rena washed her face and hands in the bowl that had belonged to her mother. Sharing all those precious memories with Scott brought her comfort.

Her child would look to her like she'd looked to her mother. Scott helped her see that. When he shared the riches of the Bible with her or pointed out the relevance of the notes her mother had written in the pages, she saw lessons that her mother hadn't had time to teach her.

But the lessons were still there to be learned.

And learn them I will.

She dried her face and went to cook supper.

While they ate, she warmed water on the stove. She asked him to take a pot of the water to her room and left the rest for him.

"I'm going to wash off the dirt from the garden and change clothes. There's enough water for you, and I dragged the tub into your room earlier."

Rena left him and closed the door to her room. She was clean and dressed in a fresh skirt and blouse when she went back into the front room. Scott was nowhere to be seen, so she went to work on the supper dishes.

The sound of a rider approaching startled her.

"Scott, someone is here." She put the dish towel down and knocked on his door. There was no answer.

Footsteps on the porch at this time of night meant he would be needed in town.

She knocked again. "Scott."

When there was still no answer, she pushed the door open. Scott was on the side of the bed, dressed in clean clothes and leaned over against the pillows. He was sound asleep. She smiled at how he could sleep with his neck bent at such a sharp angle.

A heavy knock on the door woke him. He opened his eyes and smiled. A sweet smile that he rarely used. It was unguarded and reached his eyes. He'd been peaceful in that moment. No responsibilities or need to put on a brave face.

This was the face of the authentic Scott. The man behind the work and determination. The man who teased her about her lack of homestead skills and en-joyed her cooking. This man was someone she wanted to know better.

The knocking on the door came again. "Sheriff! It's me, Eli."

The smile faded. "Just a minute." He reached for his boots. "Will you let him in?"

She invited Eli inside.

"Would you like some coffee and a piece of cake?"

Eli nodded. "That would be great. I missed supper."

Rena poured three cups of coffee.

Scott joined them at the table, and Rena served the remainder of a cake she'd made the day before.

"Sorry to disturb you folks, but there's been some trouble in town."

"Is anyone hurt?" Scott was always concerned for the people first. She admired that about him.

"Nothing needing a doctor. I imagine there'll be some bruises on a couple of fellas tomorrow, but they'll get over it." Eli put his fork on the plate. "This is mighty fine cake, Mrs. Braden."

She acknowledged him with a smile, but knew Scott wouldn't want to talk of cake right this moment.

"What happened, and who's hurt?"

"Remember I told you Jack Jefferson had hired two new hands?"

"Yes."

"They decided to spend their wages at Mabel's Saloon tonight. They made a big night of it, too. Lots of drinking and telling tales." He took another bite of cake. "They were laughing and saying how Jack Jefferson wanted only tough men to work for him. They started bragging about how they could sneak up on a fella and hit him hard enough to make him see stars."

Scott leaned forward in his chair. "These are the two you suspected of ambushing us."

"Yep. Turns out I was right. Elmer Hicks was pouring drinks behind the bar and heard them. He sent one of his girls to get me from the office. Before I could get back, a brawl had broke out. I went inside just in time to see Elmer standing on a chair behind the bar with his pistol pointed in the air. He drew back on the hammer, and you could've heard a feather fall. He cleared the place out. Made 'em all leave money on the bar to pay for the damages."

"Are the two men in jail?"

Eli shook his head. "That's the worst of it. They were gone when I got there. Someone said they started the fight and went out the back door as it was getting good."

"They must've heard Elmer send for you and started the fight as a diversion."

"That's what I figure."

Scott drained his coffee cup and stood. "Let's head over to Jefferson's ranch and see if they're crawling into the bunkhouse."

"I'll be home as soon as I can." He grabbed his hat and jacket. "Bolt the door. I'll knock when I get back."

"Be careful." She looked at Eli, too. "Both of you."

Scott threw open the bunkhouse door, and it slammed against the wall. "Good morning, gentlemen." He stood just inside the doorway, and Eli came in, followed by Jack Jefferson, Gilbert and two hands who had been on the porch outside. The last two carried lanterns and lit the room.

Groans and moans filled the air. More than one cowboy reached for a pistol.

"I wouldn't do that if I were you." Scott and Eli stood with guns drawn.

"What are you doing, Sheriff?" Gilbert wanted to know. "You rouse us all in the middle of the night for what?"

"Where are the two men you hired last, Jefferson?" Scott questioned Jack Jefferson while he surveyed the room. Eli went from bunk to bunk, looking for the two men.

"I fired them this afternoon."

Scott hadn't expected that answer. "Why?"

"Some of my men said they liked to bully. They weren't doing their jobs, but they tried to force others to do it for them. Thought they'd come on my ranch and try to boss my men." Jack Jefferson looped his thumbs in his belt. "I'm the only boss on this ranch."

Gilbert came into the middle of the room. "What do you want?"

"Those men."

"I saw them slipping out the back door of Mabel's Saloon about three hours ago. You probably couldn't catch them if you tried." Gilbert laughed. "I know why you want them now. You think they're the men who hit you in the alley."

Eli holstered his gun. "Elmer Hicks said they were bragging about it."

"I heard them. Said they could sneak up on a fella and never get caught. Then they started that brawl, and I saw them slipping out the back door."

Scott lowered his gun. "You didn't try to stop them?"

"Why? They didn't hit me in the head." Gilbert chuckled. "If you don't mind, I'm going back to bed. Daylight comes early, and some of us have work to do."

The cowboys in the bunkhouse grumbled and moaned as they settled back into their bunks.

Jack Jefferson took one of the lanterns. "Scott Braden, if you ever think about coming out here in the middle of the night again, don't do it." He walked out of the bunkhouse ahead of them.

Scott and Eli mounted up and rode off.

"Do you think we should go after them?" Eli's voice was filled with frustration.

"I don't think we'd find them. It's almost dawn. They've got a head start of several hours. They're probably miles away by now." He turned Copper toward home. "The good news is we'll probably never see them again. And with them gone, we don't have to worry about it happening again."

"I still think someone on that ranch put the idea in their head."

"I agree, Eli. But sometimes you have to let go of the trouble that's let go of you."

Chapter Fourteen

On Easter morning, Rena pinned on her new straw hat and surveyed her reflection in the mirror. Silk flowers in spring colors circled the brim. It was the perfect complement to her mint-green skirt and jacket with tiny buttons and a coordinating yellow blouse. She would love to feel pretty again. The last few days found her tired and weak. Her stamina had waned to the point she wasn't able to do all of her chores. The celebration of Easter would be a boost to her spirit. It had been in the forefront of her thoughts all week.

Scott was waiting for her on the porch when she went outside. "You look a vision this morning, Rena."

"You look handsome today, Sheriff Braden." She'd asked Opal to make him a new shirt in a blue to match his eyes. He wore it with his favorite brown leather vest. The badge on his chest was as much a part of him as his crooked smile. And she loved him.

She couldn't catch her breath. She loved him. Heat filled her face, and suddenly her breaths came in short, shallow gulps. How could she be in love with Scott? He didn't love her. This wasn't supposed to happen.

"Rena, are you okay?" He reached out to steady her. "Sit here." He led her to one of the rocking chairs on the porch. "Can I get you something? A glass of water?"

She gaped at him and nodded in a dizzy, uncertain way that was more like a bobble than a nod. He rushed into the house and came back with a glass. She took a slow, deliberate breath and reached for the glass. She watched him over the rim as she drained the glass dry.

He was handsome. No. Gorgeous. Those eyes. And that smile. That smile is what started this whole panic and revelation.

Rena Braden was in love with her husband. He didn't know it. She wouldn't tell him. Not when he'd offered his friendship and name, but nothing more.

Scott took the glass from her. "Better?"

She cleared her throat. "Yes. I'm sorry. I don't know what got into me." Well, she knew what, but not why.

"It's probably all the stress you've been under these past months." He swept his arm toward the door. "We don't have to go to church today. We can stay, and you can rest. I'll read the Bible to you, but I won't preach a sermon. That's not something I'd be comfortable doing."

He wasn't a preacher, but the way he lived and the care he showed for others impacted her life more than any sermon she'd ever heard. He was a good man.

The weight of her newly discovered love dragged her heart out of her throat and into her stomach. He was a good man. He would be her friend, but he could never love her. Not after the way she'd lived her life before their marriage.

He believed in forgiveness, and he'd never treated her unkindly. But that did not mean he would relinquish his heart to her care. She had ruined any expectation of love from a godly man when she'd abandoned her faith.

"Yes. Stress. There has been a lot of stress on us." She stood. "I would like to go to church in town today though. I can rest this afternoon. I'd like to spend Easter in the Lord's House with you and my father."

"If you're sure?"

"I am."

When he held her hand to steady her as she climbed into the wagon, she appreciated his strength with a new perspective. The deep rumble of his voice as he chatted on the drive into town was like the music of a slow dance on a moonlit night. His blue eyes sparkled under the rim of his hat when he laughed at something she said.

All the little things her heart had noticed had been tucked away in her mind without time for consideration. She didn't realize she'd memorized his face, and now she could see it when she closed her eyes.

This wouldn't do. She had to capture the strength of her devotion to him and hide it in the recesses of her heart.

During the service, Rena stood between Scott and Opal. Her father was on Opal's far side. The two of them had been keeping company since Rena's birthday. It was sweet to see her father embark on a journey to new happiness.

Rena noticed Scott's scrutiny of her more than once while the congregation sang. He was likely worried about her. She was a bit worried herself. Her heart raced at his nearness, yet the events of the morning must have taken a greater toll than she'd first thought. The room began to spin before her eyes, and her knees gave way. To keep from falling, she grabbed Scott's arm and sank onto the bench behind her.

He whispered close to her ear. "Are you okay?"

"Please. Don't make a fuss." She pushed herself up to sit straight against the back of the seat. "I don't want to disrupt the service."

Opal stooped to check on her. "Would you like me to help you outside?"

She shook her head. She would make it through the service and go home to rest afterward.

Reverend Gillis shared the story of Easter, and some of the children shared pictures they'd drawn in Bible class. It was a joyous celebration of Christ.

Rena was relieved to have made it to the final hymn and insisted that she was strong enough to stand and join in the singing. She knew it was a mistake before the song ended.

While Reverend Gillis prayed the closing prayer, she leaned against Scott. "I need to leave. Please help me to the wagon. Something is wrong." She hated to show disrespect by leaving during the prayer, but the strength in her legs was fading fast. She nudged Scott toward the aisle, and he walked with her to the door.

The preacher said the last amen when she stepped down to the first tread, and her knees buckled.

Scott pulled her close to keep her from falling to the ground. "Doc Taylor!"

The congregants spilled out of the church and formed a large circle around them, firing questions in rapid succession.

"What happened?" A voice came from behind her.

Someone else asked, "Who is it?"

"Is someone ill?" Charlotte's question echoed with concern.

"It's Rena Braden." Cyrus Busby turned to tell his wife.

Betty Alexander peered over Mr. Busby's shoulder. "I can't say I'm surprised."

Her father came into view. "Rena, dear." She hated the look of dread on his face. He'd worn that look the day her mother died and again when Rena had told him about the baby. He helped Scott lower her to sit on the church steps. Opal was close behind him.

Doc Taylor leaned and took her wrist in his fingers. "Someone seems to be a bit upset." He checked her eyes and put a hand to the side of her neck. "Do you feel sick at your stomach?"

Rena looked at those gathered around her. Some were dear friends, and their faces showed genuine concern. Others seemed eager to watch the happenings unfolding around her.

"I'll be fine, Doc." She tried to get up, but the spinning in her head prevented it.

"It's no surprise she's taken ill." Betty's voice belied the air of concern she tried to project. "In her condition."

"What are you talking about?" Papa jerked to look at Betty. He looked back at Rena. "Are you sick, child?" Her father was a gentleman who would never discuss her condition in public. He likely had no idea of the gossip that swirled around his daughter in recent weeks.

Someone near the back of the crowd laughed. "She's not sick, Grandpa!"

Rena closed her eyes in an effort to block out the faces that stared at her. It didn't help. Her secret was no longer private.

The gasps and murmurs that went through the crowd did not seem fitting.

In spite of her pain and weakness, Rena could be silent no longer. "Today is Easter. Why would we behave like this on the church grounds on the Lord's Day?"

Betty Alexander made no effort to hide her contempt for Rena. "You just came back to the church in the last few months. Who are you to tell us how to behave?"

Her energy was leaving her, but she would not allow the woman's judgment to make her feel unworthy. "God accepts me, Miss Alexander. Even if you don't."

Charlotte stepped out of the circle. "You're having a baby?" Her question was an accusation.

Rena gave a slight nod to her friend. The motion wrenched her stomach.

"You didn't tell me."

"Not likely she'd want to discuss it seeing as she's been married so recently." Betty got in her last word before she turned and walked away.

Charlotte held her arms wide. "All these people knew, but not me. Your best friend." She turned and walked away.

"Wait, Charlotte." Her effort to sit up caused a pain like none she'd ever felt. She doubled over and screamed.

Doc Taylor stood up. "That's enough. Get her to my office. I'll meet you there."

Scott lifted her in his arms and carried her to their wagon. Opal climbed in with her and held her hand. Scott drove the wagon with care and speed. In no time at all he had carried her into the doctor's examining room and left her in his care.

Opal stood by the bed and offered her assistance to the doctor.

It didn't take him long to tell her that the baby she'd felt move just yesterday was at great risk. And so was she.

Scott paced in the front room of Doc Taylor's office. Oscar sat in a chair and stared blankly out the window. Scott watched his lips move in silent prayer.

He wrung his hands, and then shoved his fingers through his hair. "What is taking so long?" It took every ounce of restraint he possessed to keep his voice low. He didn't want to disturb Rena. The gut-wrenching scream that tore from her on the church steps had been his undoing. The hour that had passed since that time seemed to drag on and on.

Oscar answered without taking his eyes from the front window. "Doc Taylor knows what he's doing. If anyone can help her, he can."

Another hour passed. All Scott could hear from the other room was Doc Taylor asking Rena questions in low tones and her sporadic groans of pain.

He went to the door of the examining room and lifted his hand to knock. It opened, and Doc Taylor shooed him back.

He came out and closed the door behind him. "She's resting. Opal will stay with her and call if she needs me."

Scott needed answers. "How is she? What's happening?"

"I'm afraid we won't know how she is for a couple of days."

"What?" His voice rose, and he clinched his fist to keep from shouting. "Why?"

"Sit down, Sheriff." Doc Taylor sat behind his desk. "Do you want Oscar to hear this, or should I ask him to leave?"

"He should know. He's her father." Scott dropped into a chair in front of the doctor's desk.

"Rena could lose the child."

"Why?" Scott knew how much she loved the babe she carried.

"From everything she's told me today, I think worry and stress have weakened her. She hasn't eaten well in the last many days."

"I'll get her to eat. I'll make sure no one bothers her. She won't see a minute of stress." He meant every word.

Doc Taylor held up his hand. "Wait, Sheriff. There's more." He rubbed the hand across his chin. His eyes were serious. "I'm afraid we may lose Rena, too. If she doesn't rest and recover from today, she could leave us."

"No." Oscar buried his face in his hands.

"Doc, you gotta do something. Anything." He pointed at the room where she rested. "I can't just sit and wait on Rena to die. I won't."

"There are complications, Sheriff. The details are something a man doesn't need to know unless he's a doctor. I promise to do my best for her, but I want her to stay here for at least two days. Opal has volunteered to sit with her."

"I'll stay with her. She's my wife."

"You can see her, but only for a couple of minutes. I won't have you upsetting her."

"I won't."

"You won't mean to, but a woman in her condition can be fragile. If we want her to have the best opportunity to come through this, we've got to use every precaution."

"I'll use caution. I won't say a word, if that's what she needs. But I will not leave her. I'll be here until you say I can take her home."

"When she goes home, she won't be able to do chores. She'll have to stay in bed until the baby comes." He paused. "If the baby makes it."

Scott hung his head. "The baby has to live."

Doc Taylor left him and Oscar and went back to Rena.

Oscar sat up straight. "Thank you for all you've done for my girl."

Scott bolted out of the chair. "I'm not through doing for your girl, Oscar. This is not the end. It can't be." He looked out the window. Most of the people who'd come by the office to wait for news had given up and gone away after the first few minutes. He had every idea they'd be by tomorrow and every day she stayed in the doctor's care.

Across the street, Reverend Gillis and his wife strolled hand in hand. Scott opened the door and called out to him. The couple crossed over to the sidewalk in front of the doctor's office.

"How is she, Sheriff?" The preacher was always kind. Scott appreciated it more than ever at this moment.

"Doc is worried. Real worried."

Mrs. Gillis reached out and patted Scott's arm. "We've been praying for that sweet girl since you brought her here."

"Thank you. She needs it." He couldn't bring himself to elaborate on the dire circumstances. "Please keep praying. For her and for the baby."

"We will. And don't you hesitate to send for me if I can help." Reverend Gillis clapped him on the shoulder. "Keep strong in your faith. She needs that from you. You promised it when you married her."

"And I meant every word." Scott nodded and closed the door as they walked away.

When Doc Taylor let him in to see Rena, he kept his promise and didn't disturb her. She lay against the white sheet with her eyes closed. He wanted to touch her hand, to offer comfort, but he didn't.

Several hours later he dozed in a chair in the front office.

Opal nudged him awake. "She wants to see you."

He went to stand by her bed, and her eyes flickered open. Is this how she felt when he'd been hurt? Helpless and vulnerable. In a way he never wanted to experience again.

She lifted her fingers, and he captured her hand in his. "I'm sorry." He leaned close to hear her whispered words. "The rumors."

"Don't you think about anything but getting well. Doc says you need to rest."

"The baby?"

He wouldn't lie to her. He didn't want to frighten her, but she deserved to know the truth. She'd shown more strength than any woman he'd known. He'd misjudged her at first. The things she'd done for her baby—and for him and her father—proved her strength.

"The baby needs you to rest."

She closed her eyes. "I'll rest then." Her words drifted away as she fell asleep.

The next two days passed with gradual improvement. He spent the hours by her bedside while she slept or in the front room of the doctor's office. More than once, Doc Taylor tried to make him leave, but he wouldn't leave until Rena did. If rest would heal her, he'd make sure she got rest.

Rena was sitting in a chair on Tuesday morning when he entered the room.

"I'm surprised to see you up." Some color had returned to her cheeks, but she was by no means well.

"I feel much stronger. The baby and I are not out of danger, but the doctor just told me I can go home today." She dropped her gaze to her hands. "If you prefer, I could stay with my father."

A light tapping drew their attention, and Opal Pennington stuck her head around the door. "How's the patient this morning?"

Scott invited her into the room. "She's been given permission to leave."

Opal smiled. "Oh, that's wonderful news."

"I have to get out of this room. The longer I'm here, the more I feel as though the walls are closing in on me. We were just discussing where I should go."

He didn't understand why this was a question. "You'll go home with me."

"I don't know, Scott."

The doctor came into the room. "I see we're already overwhelming the patient this morning."

"Doc, I have to leave. Don't make me stay."

A commotion outside the window caught Scott's eye. People moved along the street and sidewalk in the direction of his office. He pulled his watch from his vest pocket and checked the time.

"What is it?" Rena leaned forward in the chair.

Scott watched the work going on across the street. "Eli is setting up the ballot box outside my office. People will be able to start voting in a few minutes."

"I've kept you from your work. I'm sorry, Scott." Rena walked up behind him. "You go ahead. I can walk to Papa's."

He turned to her but spoke to Doc Taylor and Mrs. Pennington. "Could we have a moment alone, please?"

The two of them left and closed the door.

"Why do you want to go to your father's house?"

Rena looked at the people coming to vote. "I wouldn't think you'd want me around after all that's gone on."

"What has gone on, Rena?"

"I've caused rumors that stand to ruin you and Papa. You didn't do that, but you're bearing the brunt of it."

"We don't know the results of the rumors." He touched her face and angled it toward him.

"But I'm the one who walked away from the church. I turned my back on God and all my parents taught me. Eugene couldn't have fooled me if I hadn't been trying to live my life without God. I turned to Eugene for comfort and attention. I was trying to run from the pain of losing my mother, but in the end, it only brought more pain. And not just to me, but to Papa." She hung her head. "And you. I'll talk to Papa. He'll probably let me stay with him until the baby is born. Then I can move away and start a life with the baby where no one knows me."

He wanted her to break free of the guilt that gripped

her. "You've accepted responsibility for all you've done. Let go of the guilt. You're forgiven."

"They haven't forgiven me." She pointed at the crowd lined up outside his office. "And some of them are accusing you."

"What they think doesn't matter. What God thinks matters."

He took her hand. "I want you to come home to New Dawn Ranch with me. Regardless of the election results. I didn't promise to marry you so I could win the election. The promise I made before God was to you and the baby. Let's get you home." He looked out the window. "But I do want to vote before we head out of town." He winked and tugged her toward the door.

They walked into the front room where Doc Taylor sat behind his desk. "I want to see you in two days. Send for me at once if you see any of the symptoms I told you to watch for. There's a lot of excitement in town today. Don't let the stress of it set you back."

Mrs. Pennington gave her a quick hug. "I'll come out to your place and check on you in a few days."

"Thank you. Both of you." Rena followed Scott onto the street.

Elmer Hicks was one of the first people in line to vote. "Howdy, Sheriff. Who you voting for today?"

Several people laughed.

"Elmer, you know we do a secret ballot in Gran Colina." Scott led Rena up the steps and offered her a chair on the porch. He inspected the ballot box that Eli had put on a table with a stack of paper ballots. "Is Reverend Gillis here yet?"

"He's coming!" Mrs. Gillis called out in her sing-song voice. "He's been over at the church praying about the election."

"I know how I'm gonna vote. The preacher's prayers won't change that." Gilbert Jefferson had positioned himself near the ballot box.

"You can vote how you want, but you can't stand over the box while everyone else does." Eli moved in close and blocked Gilbert's view of the ballots.

"Who's watching you, Deputy?" Jack Jefferson called out from the bottom of the steps.

Scott pulled a chair up next to the ballot box. "The preacher is going to sit right here and watch the box. Every man will fill out his own ballot. No one will watch that part." Reverend Gillis came forward to take his seat. "The count will be done right here, in broad daylight, by the preacher after the last man votes."

Betty Alexander asked, "Since the preacher is such a good friend to Mayor Livingston and you, Sheriff, would it look better if someone else counted? Or maybe we should have two people counting. Just to keep things honest."

Reverend Gillis raised his eyebrows. "Well, folks, I knew this was a contentious election, but I didn't know I'd be the one who'd have to defend my honesty before it ended. I say we get this voting started, so we can see who will lead Gran Colina for the next two years."

Jack Jefferson stepped up onto the porch. "If it's all the same to you, Preacher, I have a problem with the sheriff and his wife standing so close to the ballot box."

Gilbert added his objection. "She's the mayor's daughter, too. It just don't look right."

Scott came forward. He'd had about all he was going to take. The accusations and not-so-subtle hints had pushed him to his limits. "What are you saying, Jefferson?"

"I'm saying that your fate is in the hands of these voters." He pointed at the crowd in the street. "You standing here might come across as a man trying to intimidate."

"If anyone has tried to use intimidation in this election, it hasn't been me." He struggled against the urge to call Jefferson out directly. "I'm still the sheriff in this town, and it's my job to stand guard over the election process."

"Preacher, what do you think?" Cyrus Busby joined the conversation.

Reverend Gillis slid a finger inside his collar. "There's been a lot more suspicion and mistrust in this election than any I've seen. I don't think it's good for the outcome. We need to be able to have conversations and share different opinions without tearing one another apart."

Betty Alexander asked, "Even when the integrity of the candidate is in question?"

That was it. Scott stepped to the edge of the porch. "Is this what we've come to? We stand in the street and accuse one another. We argue over things that we could all agree on if we liked the person doing the talking."

Rena came and stood close to him.

"People have a right to know about who they're voting for. You can't keep secrets and expect the townsfolk to trust you." The relentlessness in Betty was baffling.

"Why, Miss Alexander? Why must every detail of a body become public knowledge?"

"There are questions—rumors, if you will—that give a person cause to be concerned. Even if that person can't vote." Bitterness dripped from her words.

"Do you want to know if I'm perfect? You've talked in front of as many people as would listen about everything you had a clue about."

Cyrus Busby answered him. "You haven't been the same since you got married. You won't say why you got married so fast to a woman you didn't even seem to like before the day of the wedding." Bile didn't permeate his tone, but the accusation was there, just the same.

Rena slumped against Scott. He was afraid the stress Doc Taylor had warned them about had reached a boiling point, and she was succumbing to it. He wrapped his arm around her shoulders and steadied her. He felt her tremble against his side.

He would put an end to this now. "No, I'm not perfect, but I do my best to live a God-fearing life. I serve others and this community. So does my wife. We are a faithful part of the Gran Colina Church."

Cyrus lifted one hand. "All politicians go to church." Laughter erupted from every direction.

"That's where I'm different, Cyrus. I'm not a politician. I care about this town, and I care about you, the people of this town."

Louise Freeman joined the fray. "There's still the question of your character. Yours and your wife's." Save one or two occasions, in all the time that had passed after she'd abandoned him for Thomas Freeman, Louise had maintained a polite indifference. Today, he knew her desire to see her husband become mayor at any cost motivated her attack.

He looked out over the faces of the townsfolk. Some were angry. Some questioned. A few were embarrassed. "If you're looking for a perfect candidate— I'm not your man." Scott pointed at Gilbert. "Neither is he."

The gathered crowd rumbled in a way that indicated many were considering Gilbert as the best man for sheriff.

"Do what you want." Scott lifted a hand in surrender. "All this slander and stress has caused my wife to be ill. Being sheriff shouldn't cost anyone in my family their very life. Especially not the life of an innocent baby." Gasps came from several of the women. "Yes, Rena is expecting a baby. She is my wife. The child is mine." The words came from his heart. Rena's baby was his child. In every way that mattered.

Jack Jefferson's voice rang out over the din. "How

can we believe you? It's the day of the election. You'd say anything to get these people to vote for you."

"That's where you're wrong, Jefferson. You might say anything to gain a vote for your nephew or the banker who owes his livelihood to the money you put in his bank, but I would not."

Oscar clapped his hand on Scott's shoulder. "Don't let them get to you. He's just trying to rile you up."

"I say it's time for new leaders!" Thomas Freeman stepped forward. "You won't hear the kind of gossip and rumors about me that you've heard about this man." He pointed at Oscar. "As long as Oscar Livingston is mayor, the people who vote for him will vote for Scott Braden to be sheriff. Do you really want things in Gran Colina to go forward in the same spirit and attitude of the last few weeks?"

Shouts of agreement echoed from every direction as different people expressed their opinions.

Scott looked at Rena. Her face was pale, and her jaw was set. The pain in her eyes broke his heart anew. He leaned close and whispered to her. "Are you okay?"

"I'm so sorry, Scott." Her refusal to answer made his decision for him.

He turned back to the crowd and raised his hand for silence. A hush fell over the street. "I hereby resign as sheriff of Gran Colina. I do not wish to serve in a town where the people conduct themselves in the manner I have seen today. I won't be responsible for a town that cares more about local gossip than the lives of those living in the community."

Scott took Rena by the hand and moved toward the

steps. Without warning, she collapsed, and he scooped her up into his arms. The murmurs of concern that rippled among the people were meaningless to him. He carried her down the steps.

Doc Taylor came up beside him. "Bring her to my office."

Chapter Fifteen

Rena woke from a nap on the settee in the front room of the cabin. The sun had set, and a fire warmed the room. She pushed herself up to a sitting position.

"How do you feel?" Scott gave her a cup of tea and sat on the hearth.

"Better." She held the cup in both hands and soaked in its warmth. She looked through the open curtain. "Well, the election is over by now."

He followed her gaze with his eyes. "Yes."

"Do you regret resigning?" She leaned against the back of the settee.

"No. While you rested, I checked on the cattle and took care of the chores. I'll be able to take over the chores you've been doing. The doctor wouldn't have agreed to send you home otherwise."

"I'm sorry for the extra work."

"Without the duties of the sheriff, I'll have plenty of time."

She put her cup on the table and stood. "I know how you love protecting the people of Gran Colina."

"I did, but I've got the ranch—or the beginnings of a ranch."

Rena walked toward the stove. "Are you hungry?"

"Your dinner is under that dish towel." He pointed to where he'd set her food aside. "I ate earlier. You can sit at the table to eat, but remember Doc wants you on the settee with your feet up most of the time."

"I'll try." She sat down to eat and bowed her head in silent prayer. Before she opened her eyes, they heard a horse riding up the lane to the cabin.

Boots on the porch and a knock on the door sounded in the quietness. "Scott, it's me, Oscar." Her father kept his voice low, probably trying not to disturb her.

Scott let him inside and poured coffee for him. They both sat at the table with Rena.

"Are you feeling stronger?" Worry hung on every word.

"I am, Papa." She pointed at the ham steak and potatoes on her plate. "My husband is taking care of me."

"Good for him." Her father looked from her to Scott. "Do you want to know how the election turned out?"

She put her fork down.

Scott shook his head. "It doesn't matter. I don't want to hear anything that could upset Rena. Doc Taylor threatened my hide if I let anything else upset her before the baby is born."

"This won't upset you." Her father reached across the table and covered her hand. "The election was not close at all." His eyes began to sparkle, and she knew he'd won.

"Oh, Papa! You won!"

His smile was huge. "I did." He looked at Scott. "You did, too."

She gasped. "How?"

"That's not possible. I resigned as sheriff."

"You resigned as sheriff. You did not remove your name from the election." Papa grinned at them. "As the mayor of Gran Colina, I rejected your resignation while you took Rena to Doc Taylor. Then you won the election."

"How? When I left they were murmuring and complaining against me."

"A few were. It never ceases to amaze me that a few people can make so much noise that they sound like a majority. Then you hand them all a piece of paper and they write down their opinion. The silence of the ballot keeps one voice from carrying over another." Her father drank the last of his coffee. "Seems the silent ones in a crowd spoke with more power than the few who raised their voices."

Scott sat back in his chair. "I won't accept the position." He caught Rena's gaze and held it. "The doctor says Rena and the baby are still at risk. They could be in danger for weeks or months to come. I'll be right here with her. Since one of the major complaints from folks was my being with Rena and not always in town, I won't attempt to explain or argue. I decline."

Papa tapped a finger on the table. "Scott, don't you see? The townsfolk realize what a good man you are.

When you left, one after another told of something you'd done for them. They remember how you almost died on your first day in Gran Colina because you wouldn't sit by while someone robbed the bank of their money. They love and respect you."

Rena agreed. "And they don't even know what you'd done for me and Papa."

Her father nodded. "We agreed from the beginning that we were in this together."

"Wait a minute." She pointed at Scott. "You said that when you came out of Papa's office while I was packing my things the day after we married. What were you talking about?"

Her father answered. "We agreed to stick together through the election and do everything we could to protect the town."

Scott twisted his mouth into the smile she loved. "We agreed to keep an eye on any efforts to mislead the people or make the elections unfair. We had to protect the outcome for the future of Gran Colina. We suspected that Thomas and Gilbert were working with Jack Jefferson to win at any cost." He shot a questioning look at her father. At his nod, Scott continued. "We thought from the beginning that Jefferson had an ulterior motive, but we could find no proof."

"What could his motive be?"

Her father explained. "As sons of the founders, Eli and Jack and I watched our fathers shape this town. The power shifted back and forth over the years. Some years, a Livingston would be mayor. Others, one of the Gardners would be sheriff or mayor. The Jeffersons had times when they were included, but they spent their time and efforts building their ranch."

"Why would that matter in this election?" Rena didn't see the problem.

"Jack decided that his wealth had earned him the right to have a Jefferson in public office. Even though Gilbert's father didn't think he was cut out for leadership, Jack wanted it for him. Jack couldn't manage his ranch and be mayor or sheriff. His holdings are too large. He has money. He wanted power, or a connection to that power."

"Why didn't he run for mayor? It's easier than being the sheriff." Rena was trying to follow their thinking.

"He knows he's not well liked. Thomas Freeman is accepted. Even if folks don't like him, he wields a lot of power by owning the bank. Jack Jefferson is his biggest depositor."

"So if Jefferson helped get Thomas Freeman the election, he could put pressure to bear and make decisions for the town that suited him." She nodded. "I see, but was there anything that you found out that exposed his plan today? I've heard no word of it before this moment."

"No." Scott stood up and stretched his back. "And if we started suggesting or hinting at our theory, the only result would be to insult or slander them. We couldn't do to them what they were doing to us."

"The people have spoken, just the same." Papa came to kiss her on the cheek. "You get better. Rest. Take care of my grandchild."

"Be careful on the ride back to town." Scott opened the door.

"I'll see to it that Eli handles your duties until you can come back to town." Her father stepped onto the porch.

"I meant what I said, Oscar. My place is here, taking care of Rena."

"We'll see." Papa waved and stepped off the porch into the night.

The next morning, Charlotte came to visit. She drove her father's wagon and pulled up to the cabin. Rena was sitting in a rocker on the porch with her feet propped on the bottom of the railing. She tied off a row of stitching on the baby quilt and dropped it into her lap.

Charlotte grabbed a basket from the wagon seat and shaded her eyes from the morning sun. "Can a friend bring a peace offering?"

"A friend doesn't need to. All that's needed is her presence." She was delighted to see Charlotte. "I'd come to you, but if you'll look there by the corral, you'll see my guardian. I'm not allowed to leave the chair or the porch."

Charlotte came up the steps and put the basket on the table by Rena's chair. She leaned in for a hug.

"Pull that chair closer and sit with me." Rena thanked her for the basket of goodies.

"Momma was in a baking mood last night. There were pies all over the kitchen this morning. I brought two."

"I'm so sorry, Charlotte." Rena didn't want to dance around the reason her friend hadn't been nearby in the last few days. "I hadn't told anyone about the baby. Several people guessed, but the only people I told were Papa and Scott."

Charlotte watched Scott fill the water trough in the corral. "I heard the rumors on election day."

"They're awful."

"Is that why you didn't tell? Because of what people might say."

"There were a lot of reasons, Charlotte, but none of them was meant to hurt you."

"I know." Charlotte turned to face her. "If I were to be honest with you, I'd say I'm a bit jealous. You have everything I want. A husband," She pointed at Scott. "A home and a baby coming. Your life is perfect."

Rena wanted to weep for Charlotte's innocence. "Nothing is perfect."

Charlotte stayed with her for another hour. Rena showed her the quilt and took her inside to see the cradle. Scott had finished it and placed it in the corner of the front room.

Rena hugged Charlotte on the front porch. "Thank you for coming. Your friendship is very important to me. I'm sorry I hurt you."

"I'm happy to see you. I'll be praying for you and the baby."

Scott looked across the yard. "Rena, please rest." Rena waved and sat in her chair.

"It may not be perfect, but your life sure is nice." Charlotte grinned and left her.

Rena watched the wagon drive up the lane. She had to agree with Charlotte.

Scott worked on the barn door now. Two of the boards had worked loose, and he was hammering them back into place.

The love she felt for him overflowed in her heart. He'd refused to let her leave. He'd given up his position as sheriff to care for her.

Her life was indeed very nice.

She picked up the quilt to work on the next stitches. A rider galloped onto the lane and slowed as he neared the barn. It was Eli Gardner.

"Whoa." He pulled the reins and dismounted. "Morning, Mrs. Braden." He lifted his hat to her.

"Good morning. What brings you to the New Dawn Ranch?" She loved saying the name. The hope in the words comforted her every time.

He took a step toward the barn and Scott. "Just came to talk to your husband for a few minutes." He kept his hat in hand and backed away from her. "Nothing for you to worry about."

"If you don't want me to worry, you shouldn't act like that."

Scott dropped his hammer into the toolbox at his feet and brushed the dirt from his hands with a handkerchief. "You may as well come sit on the porch and talk in front of her. She'll worry more if we hide something from her."

The two of them joined her on the porch.

"Coffee?" Scott offered.

"No. I can only stay a minute." Eli looked at Rena.

"Are you certain it won't upset you for me to talk sheriff business?"

"No. My husband is right. I'd worry more if I had to wonder what was being said."

Eli nodded and spoke to Scott. "The trial is tomorrow. Judge Sawyer is coming in on the afternoon train today."

Her heart tightened. She'd thought Vernon Ramsey guilty from the outset, but Scott had taught her to look deeper. The man had convinced her of his claim that he only fired his gun to keep Gordon Dixon from killing him first.

"Sheriff, I know you don't want to leave your missus until the danger has passed, but would you be willing for someone to stay with her so you could come to the trial? Opal Pennington has volunteered. There's a lot at stake for Vernon Ramsey. It might sway the judge if you were there. Some of the men said they'll come take care of your animals and chores while you're in town."

"I'm not the sheriff, Eli."

"You may not be coming to the office these days, but you're the sheriff. The whole town says so. I lost count of how many folks came by to see if you were in the office. They were all right quick to point out that I didn't need to get used to sitting behind your desk. They're determined to do whatever it takes to get you back on the job."

Eli's words restored her faith in the people of Gran Colina. "Scott, you have to go. It would be terrible for Mr. Ramsey to be found guilty. The judge would listen to you."

Scott looked at her. "I can't leave you alone."

"Opal will be here." She smiled. "I'll be fine."

After Eli left, Scott and Rena sat at the table for lunch. She encouraged him to reconsider his position as sheriff. "You married me to protect your position for the sake of the town. Please don't let that go. I've cost you more than you promised. Isn't it enough that you've given up your freedom for my sake? Can't you do the work that you love? You could grow to resent me if you don't. I couldn't bear that."

He gave her one of his crooked smiles. "You drive a hard bargain, Mrs. Braden. I'll go to the trial." He took his dishes to the basin and came back for hers. "And I'll pray about the position as sheriff."

Scott arrived in town early the next morning. He wanted to see the judge and Vernon Ramsey before the trial began.

"Sheriff, you came. I wasn't sure you would." Vernon leaned his arms through the bars of his cell.

"I felt like I owed it to you. My wife insisted I come." He passed a clean shirt through the bars to him. "She sent this for you to wear, too."

"Thank her for me. She's been nothing but kind." Even a man whose life was hanging in the balance appreciated the value of Rena.

She was kind. Scott smiled at the thought.

Vernon changed his shirt, and Scott let him out of the cell. They walked to the church. Scott hated to hold the trial in the place where they worshipped, but there was no larger building in Gran Colina. If he decided to come back to the sheriff's job, he'd talk to Oscar about Thomas Freeman's idea for a town square. Maybe they could even build a courthouse on the corner across the street from the bank.

Inside the church, Scott had Vernon sit on the front bench. They were the first to arrive. A table had been set up in the front of the aisle for the judge's use.

The door opened, and Eli Gardner came in with Judge Solomon Sawyer. He was an unconventional sort. Scott had found him to be fair when he'd dealt with a thief who'd stolen from Scott's sister last year.

"Good morning, Judge Sawyer." Scott offered the judge a chair.

"Sheriff Braden." The judge sat behind the table. "I'm sorry it took me so long to get here for such a serious matter. The delay was unavoidable."

"I was grateful for the extra time to investigate this case. Though I can't say I'm pleased with the results."

The judge looked at Vernon Ramsey. "I find these cases to be the most difficult. One man is dead, and another man's life will be forever changed today."

"I'm not convinced he's guilty."

Judge Sawyer held up a hand. "I'll hear the details during the trial. I want to get both sides from the witnesses."

"What if there are no witnesses to one side?" Scott had to ask.

"That will be a shame, Sheriff. A shame that can't be helped."

It didn't take long for the church to fill with anyone who could find their way into town to watch the trial.

Scott spoke to Vernon a final time before the proceedings got underway. "If there is anything you can think of or remember that might possibly help you, please tell me."

"I've told you everything I know." Hope had faded from his eyes. Deep sorrow took its place.

"When it's time to tell your side of things, tell the judge everything that happened. Don't leave anything out." He put a hand on Vernon's shoulder. "I have to be able to tell my wife that we did everything we could to find the truth."

He nodded. "I will."

Judge Sawyer ran his courtroom with strong emphasis on getting to the truth. He did not tolerate any assumptions or guesses. If a witness had not seen something with their own eyes, he instructed the jury that it was not reliable testimony.

All the witnesses Scott had interviewed told their stories. To a man, they'd seen Vernon Ramsey sit across from Gordon Dixon and shoot him dead with a gun he held under the table.

Judge Sawyer listened intently to each one.

Vernon Ramsey took the stand just before lunch.

The judge listened to all the questions and answers. Then he asked Vernon to tell his account of what happened. "Tell it to me without interruption. I find that sometimes the details fade away when you're interrupted by questions."

Vernon told the story to the judge the same way

he'd told it to Scott and Rena—and anyone else who stood within earshot of him during the last two and a half months. He gave every detail that Scott had researched. It would come down to the jury. With no one to validate his account, Scott didn't see a way for the man to avoid the gallows. The thought was unbearable.

Judge Sawyer studied the notes he'd made during the testimony of all the witnesses.

"Mr. Ramsey, you say there was someone behind you stirring up the dead man's anger."

"Yes, sir." He looked down. "But I had only arrived on the afternoon train. I don't know the folks of this town. I couldn't point him out to you, because I heard him, but I couldn't see him."

"Do you think this witness may have seen the gun you say you heard Gordon Dixon using?"

"He'd have been close enough. I think." Vernon's voice quivered. The strain he was under was telling.

The back door of the church slammed open, and Amos Henderson entered.

Gilbert Jefferson stood by the door. He took Amos by the arm. "Get out of here, boy. There's a trial going on in here."

"That's the voice!" Vernon Ramsey pointed at Gilbert. "He's the man who was behind me in the saloon."

Alfred Murray jumped to his feet and pointed at Gilbert. "I saw... I saw you from my barber...my barbershop. You hid—" His nervousness caused his words to come slowly. "You put something under the saloon, the porch."

Gilbert shouted, "Shut up, Alfred! You don't know anything."

It seemed everyone in the room was talking at once.

Scott looked at Judge Sawyer. He kept his voice low. "If there's a gun hidden under that porch, what would you do?"

"I'd have to dismiss the case. You can't hang a man for defending himself."

"I'm sure they'll find a gun. Alfred Murray never speaks up like that. He wouldn't have interrupted your court for anything less than the truth."

"I expect you're right." Judge Sawyer banged his gavel amidst the chaos of the room.

Eli was right beside Scott. "I'll go look now." He took Alfred Murray with him.

Jack Jefferson shook his head. He walked by Gilbert on his way out of the church. "Can't you do anything right?"

"I did what you wanted. I showed people that Scott Braden ain't fit to be sheriff."

Thomas Freeman scoffed. "You proved to the entire town that you will never be sheriff again. No matter how many times you run. And you've probably ruined my chances of ever being the mayor." He led his wife toward the door.

Amos pulled out of Gilbert's grip and pushed through the people who were leaving to the front of the room. "Doc Taylor, come quick! Sheriff, it's your wife." As soon as he said the words, he spun around and left.

Scott ran down the aisle of the church after Amos.

Amos was on his horse when Scott got outside. "Hurry, Sheriff! I think it's bad. All I heard was a scream. Then Mrs. Pennington yelled for me to run for the doctor and to get you, too."

Scott ran to Copper and vaulted into the saddle. The fast horse passed Amos and the doctor on the way to the ranch.

Please, God, let her and the baby be safe. Don't let me lose her. I couldn't bear it.

He was off the horse and up the porch steps before Copper came to a halt.

"Where is she?"

Opal Pennington stood in the doorway to Rena's room. "She's in here, but I think you should let the doctor see about her before you go in."

"What happened?" He slid both hands into his hair and clinched his fists.

Doc Taylor came in before Opal could answer. She followed the doctor into Rena's room and closed the door, blocking Scott from seeing his wife or knowing her condition.

He paced the floor and prayed while the doctor tended to his wife in the other room. Oscar arrived and sat at the table, watching him.

Scott groaned. "I shouldn't have left her here. I won't be able to live if anything happens to her or the baby."

"You're in love with her." Oscar voiced a truth Scott had refused to acknowledge.

"I am." He ran his hands through his hair and laughed. "I am!"

Rena cried out in the bedroom. The breath rushed out of him, and he knocked on the door.

"I need to come in, Doc. I can't wait out here another minute."

The doctor gave his permission.

Scott rushed to her side and fell to his knees by the bed. He rested his palm on her temple and smoothed back the damp tresses from her gleaming face. All he could manage was a whisper as he heard the doctor and Opal leave the room and close the door.

"I love you." He shook his head, and laughter—uncontrollable joy—rose from his chest. "I love you, Rena."

Tears spilled from her lashes and ran down her face. "Are you sure?"

He nodded and caressed her cheek. "I've never been more sure of anything in my life. It's the strongest feeling I've ever known."

A hesitancy filled her eyes. "What about the baby?"

"I love our baby, too."

She took his hand in hers and traced his knuckles with her fingertips. "Doc says the baby will be fine." She let out a slow breath that troubled him.

"But you cried out in pain."

"The baby will be fine." A smile curved her lips. "I, on the other hand, will need a few days to recover from falling over the rug in front of the fireplace. I hit the hearth on the way down. I have a nasty bruise on my leg that hurt when the doctor was checking for a break. Thankfully, he didn't find one. I'll be fine, too."

"Our baby will be fine." Scott rested his hand on

her swollen middle and was rewarded with a strong kick. Scott smiled so big it hurt his face. He leaned forward and touched his forehead to hers. He kissed her nose and then her soft mouth, a sweet kiss she returned. The moment seared into his memory for all eternity.

"I want you to know how grateful I am that you are my wife. And that this child is mine. In the eyes of the law, and of God—and in my eyes. You never have to doubt my commitment to you or our child."

Rena's eyes filled with tears. "I don't deserve you. I'm not good enough."

Scott wrapped her in his arms. "Never say that again. I meant it when I told the people at the election that no one is perfect. I'm not perfect. You're not perfect. Remember the Scripture in Romans that tells us there is no condemnation to those that are in Christ."

She smiled through her tears. "That's one of the verses Momma underlined in her Bible. It has brought me great comfort."

He pulled her closer and rested his cheek against hers. "I will tell you one thing that I've learned. We are perfect." He kissed her cheek and then her temple. "For each other." The scent of her overwhelmed him. It was more than the floral perfume she wore. It was the fragrance of her being. The delightful aroma of a beautiful soul.

"I love you, Scott. Maybe from the time you pushed me under a desk to protect me from bank robbers." She smiled and, with her free hand, brushed his jawline.

Then she giggled. A sound he'd longed to hear from her in the months since they'd married.

He sought her lips and captured them with his. The kiss was a promise. A promise of love and faithfulness. A promise he made with his heart. A promise she returned with hers.

Epilogue

Three months later, Scott entered Rena's bedroom as Doc Taylor left. "Congratulations, Sheriff. You've got a healthy wife and baby." He clapped Scott on the shoulder. "Take care of them." Scott nodded and walked farther into the room. The doctor grinned. "I'll see myself out."

"Thank you, Doc." Scott said the words, but his focus was on Rena and his child.

He sat on the edge of her bedside, and with great care, hoping not to disturb the bundle in her arms, he whispered, "You are more beautiful than any woman I've ever seen."

Rena welcomed the gentle kiss he dropped on her lips.

"How are you?"

"Very tired." Her eyes left his and fell on the child in her arms. "And blissfully happy."

"An answer to my prayers." He put a hand on her shoulder and marveled at all God had done to bless them. To see Rena happy at the end of a year that had changed everything in their world was more than he'd imagined possible in the early days of their marriage.

She interrupted his thoughts. "Don't you want to know if the baby is a boy or a girl?"

"It doesn't matter. Boy or girl. The only thing I prayed for was life for you and the baby." He took in the sight of the child resting in her arms. The small face was perfect.

Rena pulled the quilt away from the baby's chin. "Her name is Cordelia Grace."

"After our mothers." Tears filled his eyes as Rena passed the tiny girl to him. "Hello, Cordelia. I'm your pa."

"I'm so thankful for all you've done for me and Cordelia. In the beginning, I wondered if I should leave Gran Colina and spare my father the shame of my actions. Your forgiveness and acceptance taught me how to forgive myself."

He shifted the baby to one arm and took Rena's hand. "If you'd left town, your father would have been shamed. People would have discovered the reason." He squeezed her hand. "Now he can be proud of you and the family you've made. Cordelia didn't come from me." He brushed a kiss across the top of the baby's head. "She came to me." He gazed deeply into Rena's eyes. "I'm proud to be her pa." He studied the baby's face for a moment. "She looks just like you." He lifted his eyes. "Beautiful."

"She truly is." Rena beamed at their child. "I want to be the kind of mother that Momma was to me. She would know things without being told. She loved and protected me until the day she passed. I don't know if I can be that kind of mother. What if I fail?"

Scott smiled at her. "Be the mother your mother was, and later, when Cordelia is older, you can teach her all the things you learned after your mother was gone."

He pulled her hand to his lips and kissed her knuckles. He leaned to rest his cheek against hers and drank in the joy of his family, huddled together in a circle of love. Rena lifted her hand to his face, and he prayed for them.

"Lord, thank You for the precious gift of life and family. Thank You for Cordelia." He held tighter to Rena's hand. "Thank You for the forgiveness and love You have blessed us with. Help us to live every moment to the full and honor You. We are forever grateful."

Rena took Cordelia's hand in hers.

Scott drank in the sight of his wife. "Your father saved my life the day he asked me to marry you."

Rena smiled. "And you saved mine."

Scott loved her beyond words. "You saved my heart. You made it whole again." The baby stirred in his arms. "And now Cordelia has stolen it away again."

* * * * *

If you enjoyed HUSBAND BY ARRANGEMENT,
look for these other Love Inspired Historical titles
by Angel Moore.

CONVENIENTLY WED
THE MARRIAGE BARGAIN
THE RIGHTFUL HEIR

Find more great reads at www.LoveInspired.com

Dear Reader,

Sometimes forgiving yourself is the hardest thing to do.

Thank you for reading *Husband by Arrangement*. I hope you enjoyed this story of restoration to a relationship with God. Abandoning her faith made Rena vulnerable and brought pain to her and those she loved. The faith and patience of a loving man make this story a favorite of mine.

Rena accepts responsibility for her actions. She even accepts God's forgiveness but struggles to forgive herself.

Facing the consequences of our actions on a daily basis can lead to guilt. God wants us to be repentant. Then He forgives, and He wants us to forgive ourselves.

I'd love to hear from you. You can reach me through my website at angelmoorebooks.com. You'll find the latest news and links to connect with me on social media.

May God bless and help you to forgive yourself and others.

Angel Moore

We hope you enjoyed this story from
Love Inspired® Historical.

Love Inspired® Historical is coming to
an end but be sure to discover more
inspirational stories to warm your heart
from **Love Inspired®** and
Love Inspired® Suspense!

Love Inspired stories show that
faith, forgiveness and hope have the power
to lift spirits and change lives—always.

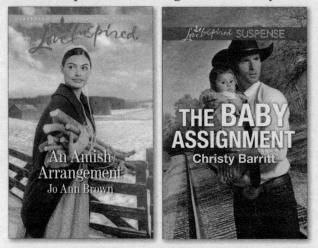

Look for six new romances every month
from **Love Inspired®** and
Love Inspired® Suspense!

COMING NEXT MONTH FROM
Love Inspired® Historical

Available April 3, 2018

THE RANCHER INHERITS A FAMILY
Return to Cowboy Creek • by Cheryl St. John

Rancher Seth Halloway is stunned when he inherits three sons from a recently deceased friend, but with the help of Marigold Brewster, the lovely new local schoolteacher, he settles into fatherhood. When the boys decide to become matchmakers, though, will he and Marigold find love?

MONTANA LAWMAN RESCUER
Big Sky Country • by Linda Ford

When Sheriff Jesse Hill rescues Emily Smith and a little boy after a stagecoach robbery, the woman can't remember anything but her name and that of the child. Now, while searching for the robbers and waiting for Emily's memory to return, he must resist falling for her.

MAIL-ORDER BRIDE SWITCH
Stand-In Brides • by Dorothy Clark

Fleeing a forced betrothal, socialite Virginia Winterman swaps places with Garret Stevenson's mail-order bride. But Garret needs a wife in name only to help in his new hotel... and Virginia hasn't worked a day in her life. Despite their differences, can she prove to him that she's his perfect match?

THE UNCONVENTIONAL GOVERNESS
by Jessica Nelson

If Henrietta Gordon wants to save enough money to reach her dream of becoming a doctor, she needs work—and Dominic, Lord St. Raven, needs a governess for his recently orphaned niece. It's a temporary arrangement, but the longer she stays, the more tempting it is to make it permanent.

LIHCNM0318

Get 2 Free Books,
Plus 2 Free Gifts—
just for trying the Reader Service!

LI17R3

SPECIAL EXCERPT FROM

Love Inspired HISTORICAL

When rancher Seth Halloway inherits a trio of orphaned boys, he has nowhere to turn—except to lovely schoolteacher Marigold Brewster. Together, they'll learn to open their hearts to new family...and new love.

Read on for a sneak preview of
THE RANCHER INHERITS A FAMILY
by *Cheryl St. John*, *the touching beginning of the series* **RETURN TO COWBOY CREEK**.

"Mr. Halloway." The soft voice near his side added to his disorientation. "Are you in pain?"

Ivory-skinned and hazel-eyed, with a halo of red-gold hair, the woman from the train came into view. She had only a scrape on her chin as a result of the ordeal. "You fared well," he managed.

"I'm perfectly fine, thank you."

"And the children?"

"They have a few bumps and bruises from the crash, but they're safe."

He closed his eyes with grim satisfaction.

"I'm Marigold Brewster. Thank you for rescuing me."

"I'm glad you and your boys are all right."

"Well, that's the thing…"

His head throbbed and the light hurt. "What's the thing?"

"They're not my boys."

"They're not?"

"I never saw them before I boarded the train headed for Kansas."

"Well, then—"

"They're yours."

With his uninjured hand, he touched his forehead gingerly. Had that blow to his head rattled his senses? No, he hadn't lost his memory. He remembered what he'd been doing before heading off to the wreckage. "I assure you I'd know if I had children."

"Well, as soon as you read this letter, along with a copy of a will, you'll know. It seems a friend of yours by the name of Tessa Radner wanted you to take her children upon her death."

Tessa Radner? "She's dead?"

"This letter says she is. I'm sorry. Did you know her?"

Remembering her well, he nodded. They'd been neighbors and classmates in Big Bend, Missouri. He'd joined the infantry alongside her husband, Jessie, who had been killed in Northern Virginia's final battle. Seth winced at the magnitude of senseless loss.

Seth's chest ached with sorrow and sympathy for his childhood friend. But sending her beloved babies to *him*? She must have been desperate to believe he was her best choice. What was he going to do with them?

Don't miss
THE RANCHER INHERITS A FAMILY
by Cheryl St.John, available April 2018 wherever
Love Inspired® Historical books and ebooks are sold.

www.LoveInspired.com

Looking for inspiration in tales
of hope, faith and heartfelt romance?

Check out **Love Inspired**® and
Love Inspired® **Suspense** books!

New books available every month!

CONNECT WITH US AT:

Harlequin.com/Community

 Facebook.com/HarlequinBooks

 Twitter.com/HarlequinBooks

 Instagram.com/HarlequinBooks

Pinterest.com/HarlequinBooks

ReaderService.com